**The Island Clinic**

*Savi...*

Welcome to par... ...
the Caribb... ...
home to chief of s... ...rivate
hospital, The I... ...ith the motto
"We are *always* here to help," The Island Clinic
was created as both a safe haven for the
rich and famous to receive medical treatment
*and* a lifeline for the local community.

This summer, we're going to meet
The Island Clinic's medical team as they work hard
to save lives…and, just maybe, get a shot at love!

*How to Win the Surgeon's Heart*
by Tina Beckett

*Caribbean Paradise, Miracle Family*
by Julie Danvers

*The Princess and the Pediatrician*
by Annie O'Neil

*Reunited with His Long-Lost Nurse*
by Charlotte Hawkes

Available now!

Dear Reader,

Of course, I've never been to St. Victoria—
the fictional island from where my heroine, Talia,
hails—but she has certainly made me fall for her
homeland!

It was incredibly good fun to write about this
beautiful island, with its volcanoes and rain forests
and those seas of turquoise blue. In my head, it is
perfectly glorious weather every day.

So where better to turn up the heat on my heroine
and hero, Talia and Liam, who lost their way years
ago when they lost each other? I loved finding out
how they were going to make their way back to one
another.

I hope you enjoy reading Talia and Liam's story as
much as I enjoyed writing it!

I love hearing from my readers, so feel free to drop
by my website at www.charlotte-hawkes.com or
pop over on Facebook or Twitter, @chawkesuk.

I can't wait to meet you.

*Charlotte* x

# REUNITED WITH HIS LONG-LOST NURSE

CHARLOTTE HAWKES

Special thanks and acknowledgment are given to
Charlotte Hawkes for her contribution to
The Island Clinic miniseries.

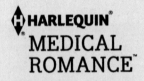

# HARLEQUIN®
## MEDICAL ROMANCE™

Recycling programs
for this product may
not exist in your area.

ISBN-13: 978-1-335-40870-9

Reunited with His Long-Lost Nurse

Copyright © 2021 by Harlequin Books S.A.

This edition published by arrangement with Harlequin Books S.A.

For questions and comments about the quality of this book, please contact us at CustomerService@Harlequin.com.

Harlequin Enterprises ULC
22 Adelaide St. West, 40th Floor
Toronto, Ontario M5H 4E3, Canada
www.Harlequin.com

**Printed in U.S.A.**

Born and raised on the Wirral Peninsula in England, **Charlotte Hawkes** is mom to two intrepid boys who love her to play building block games with them, and who object loudly to the amount of time she spends on the computer. When she isn't writing—or building with blocks—she is company director for a small Anglo/French construction firm. Charlotte loves to hear from readers, and you can contact her at her website: charlotte-hawkes.com.

### Books by Charlotte Hawkes

#### Harlequin Medical Romance

##### *Royal Christmas at Seattle General*
*The Bodyguard's Christmas Proposal*

##### *Reunited on the Front Line*
*Second Chance with His Army Doc*
*Reawakened by Her Army Major*

##### *A Summer in São Paolo*
*Falling for the Single Dad Surgeon*

*A Surgeon for the Single Mom*
*The Army Doc's Baby Secret*
*Unwrapping the Neurosurgeon's Heart*
*Surprise Baby for the Billionaire*
*The Doctor's One Night to Remember*

Visit the Author Profile page at Harlequin.com.

To my beautiful boys.

You may never read my books—trust me, you may *never* read them…understand?—but I love reading your stories about the time-traveling, space-bending rainbows!

I love you…to infinity.

Xxx

**Praise for
Charlotte Hawkes**

"Ms. Hawkes has delivered a really good read in this book where I smiled a lot because of the growing relationship between the hero and heroine… The romance was well worth the wait because of the building sexual tension between the pair."

—*Harlequin Junkie* on
*A Surgeon for the Single Mom*

# CHAPTER ONE

LIAM MILLER HAD earned his nickname, The Heart Whisperer, because his extraordinary surgical skill could coax even the most damaged patients' hearts back to a perfect, normal sinus rhythm.

It was therefore ironic, he considered, that he'd been battling his own abnormally erratic heartbeat ever since arriving on the stunning island of St Victoria a few hours earlier. Or, more accurately, ever since his seaplane had flown over the stunning three-hundred-square-mile volcanic Caribbean island.

The views were practically spellbinding, from the emerald green of its rainforest canopy to its breath-taking turquoise waters where the light seemed to burst joyously off the coral reefs and sand.

But he would not allow himself to be bewitched.

Even on the short taxi drive from the port to the renowned Island Clinic, Liam had been captivated by the sheer colour and jubilation that pulsed around the island. It was so exuberant, so vibrant.

And it was so *her*.

He tried to push the thought from his head—the way he'd kept memories of her at bay for almost three years—but suddenly, now, he couldn't seem to hold them back. Whether it was the jet-lag, or the fact that he was actually here on her homeland, Liam couldn't be sure; all he knew was that this entire island was everything she'd once described to him. And it epitomised her flawlessly.

*Talia.*

The woman who had burst into his life a little over three years ago like a spectacular rainbow striking through the dark clouds that he hadn't realised, until that point, had been so very cheerless. She hadn't simply brought colour into his cold life but rather she had pitched it resplendently all over every single wall and surface in his hitherto bleak, grey world.

She had been the very essence of fun and laughter, and she'd breathed life into his very soul. He hadn't realised it immediately, but that black, heavy, icy thing that had squatted so heavily on his chest his whole life had begun, bit by bit, to thaw.

She was the woman who had made him think, against everything his cruel and hateful father had drilled into him his entire life, that far from being to blame, he might actually be as much a victim of his mother's death as his grief-stricken father had been. She was the woman who'd let him believe that perhaps he wasn't as damaged and broken and destructive as he'd always thought. That he might just be worthy of being loved for who he was.

And then, just as abruptly as she'd surged into his life, she'd left. And with her departure every bit of that colour and joy had drained from his life. Only this time it had been even worse because he'd known what he was missing.

With a snort of irritation Liam jerked his head from the huge picture window that made up one wall of the chief of staff's office at The Island Clinic, offering magnificent views. Instead he dropped his gaze to his electronic tablet and the patient file that stared at him from the screen as he waited for Nate Edwards to return.

It galled him that he hadn't yet managed to banish thoughts of Talia Johnson from his head, even all these years later. But, he reminded himself irritably, he wasn't on St Victoria to allow memories he'd tried to bury long ago to be stirred up.

He was simply here for the patients. In particular, Lucy Wells, the fifteen-year-old girl with a congenital heart problem who needed a full aortic arch reconstruction. And he didn't really have to read the notes on his tablet again, if he was honest. He'd been living and breathing this challenging case ever since the phone call the previous week from the clinic's chief of staff, Nate Edwards.

The way he did with every one of his cases—because they all mattered. They would be lying on his OR table, and the very least they deserved was that he knew their case inside out, upside down, and every way in between. Because every one of them could be someone's child, someone's husband, someone's mother—just like his own mother had once been.

The last place she'd ever been and the first place he'd ever been.

The start of his life but the end of hers. The cruellest twist of fate for which his distraught father had never forgiven him.

Never.

Which was why he had spent his entire surgical career doggedly determined that he would save every life he possibly could.

As if saving his patients' lives could somehow make up for his birth having been the reason for his mother losing hers.

As though there was a magic number that—when he achieved it—would suddenly, magically, absolve him. Maybe it would free him of the torment, and instantly lift all that icy numbness. The way he'd once naively imagined Talia had been starting to do.

*Enough!*

He would only be here for a few weeks, a month at the most, filling in for The Island Clinic's permanent cardiothoracic surgeon following a minor boating accident—not just for the Lucy Wells case, or the several other patients awaiting surgery, but for any emergencies—but then he would be gone.

It might not be a huge island, but it was big enough. He wasn't going to see Talia here. He didn't even know for sure that she'd returned to St Victoria after she'd disappeared, without a word, from his own life. But even if she had, he wasn't about to bump into her.

He could still recall the passion in her voice as she'd described to him her job at the local hospital, across the island towards the more populated area near the capital, Williamtown, but The Island Clinic was isolated. The perfect safe haven for A-listers needing medical treatment in an environment where their privacy could be absolutely assured.

No, he wasn't going to bump into Talia here.

Which was, he assured himself firmly, exactly the way he wanted it.

'Hello, Talia. I can't say I ever expected—or hoped—to see you again.'

A shiver started on the back of Talia's neck and shot over her skin, permeating every inch of her goose-bumped flesh, through to her veins, turning her blood to ice. She couldn't turn around. She could barely even lay the last of the instruments in the metal preparation tray.

Her mind spun.

The voice was Liam's, and yet it wasn't. She recognised the clipped, unerringly professional tone yet there was also an uncharacteristic hint of ice about it that almost made her want to pull her scrubs tighter around herself. Though whether more for warmth or for protection, she couldn't quite be sure.

So he had actually come to St Victoria. Even though she'd known it was happening—even though she was the one who had put Liam's name forward to her chief of staff—she hadn't quite believed it. She'd been almost convinced he would turn down the case just because it was on St Victoria.

The fact that he hadn't only proved one thing... that she was so insignificant to him that she hadn't even factored into his decision-making process. A fact she already knew, of course. She'd discovered that three years ago. To her detriment.

Which was all the more reason why it should make no difference to her whatsoever that he was here, Talia reminded herself desperately.

She hadn't recommended Liam to Nate because she'd wanted to see him again—because she absolutely had *not*—she had simply recommended him because she'd known that Duke Hospital's famous Heart Whisperer would be the best chance for her young, desperate patient.

Her own emotions hadn't factored into the equation at all.

*Not at all.*

So why was her body trembling as though it didn't believe her?

*You're immune to him,* she reminded herself desperately, preparing to turn around as she pretended that she didn't feel half as shaky as she did.

Her one consolation was that at least Liam would never know it had been her who had put his name forward. She had asked Nate to keep that part to himself.

'Is this what you intend to do for the next month, then?' His low voice reverberated softly around the room, but she wasn't fool enough to believe that made it no less dangerous to her. 'Pretend you can't even hear me? Only I can't imagine it's going to be the most successful play you could make.'

'Of course not,' she murmured, taking one final, steadying breath before she spun around—a bright, if uncharacteristically tight, smile plastered to her lips. It promptly froze in place the moment she met his expression of cool appraisal.

Pain slammed into her, hard and unyielding.

This was the man who had taught her what it was to ache, need, sear, just with a look. With a *word.* Yet right now he was looking at her as though he didn't know her at all.

Like she was no one more special than a

stranger he was meeting for the first time. It hurt more than she could have ever imagined possible.

'Liam,' she choked out, the name seeming to stick in her mouth, as though she was trying to savour it just a fraction longer.

It was enough to make her despair of herself, especially when her eyes locked with his and she was unable to drag them away again. Dark and foreboding.

Yet it wasn't just that expression that was proving her undoing. As Talia found herself struggling for breath, fearing her legs would actually buckle beneath her, she reached behind her and gripped the medical trolley for support.

She'd spent the past three years telling herself that her girlish memories had built Liam up into something far more potent than he could ever truly have been in reality. Yet right now she realised that even her memories hadn't gone far enough.

The man was as glorious as he'd ever been. From the six-two frame outlined with those broad shoulders, down the unmistakably honed chest beneath that immaculate suit shirt—in spite of the eighty-five-degree St Victoria heat, Talia could see that nothing had changed. His square jaw was a study in masculinity, and so sharp that she thought it would cut her even from that distance. His thighs still so impossibly muscled that she practically wanted to lick them.

She swallowed. Hard.

Yep, forget the dulled memory. If anything, he seemed even more chiselled than ever and his face looked as though it had been hewn from pure granite as he glowered at her. She pretended it didn't feel like a tight fist closing around her already fragile heart.

'Is that all you have to say?' His tone was too neutral, his expression giving nothing away. 'My name? You're not even going to explain what I'm doing out here?'

Panic shot through her in an instant, and it was all Talia could do not to show it.

*He doesn't know*, she reminded herself feverishly. *He can't possibly know.*

She tried to dredge up another smile but it was impossible, she'd have to content herself with a controlled tone. One that didn't betray just how crazily she was shaking inside.

'You're here to take over one of Isak's clinical trial surgeries, I believe,' she managed. 'I'm sure that's what the rumour mill said, anyway.'

His already cold expression changed abruptly, becoming even more closed off than ever. The fist around her heart squeezed tighter. He'd gone from talking to her to shutting her out in an instant. A stark reminder of why she'd made that impossible decision, three years ago, to walk away from the only man she had ever loved.

Three years, two months, two weeks and four days, if she was going to be precise.

Shamefully, she knew it to pretty much the hour, too.

'"That's what the rumour mill said"?' he echoed. 'Is this some game you're now playing?'

The question rasped over her skin, scraping against old wounds she'd told herself were long since healed. Yet now, with a few words from Liam, they felt as raw as they had three years ago.

Leaving Duke's—leaving *him*—had been the most agonising decision of her life. Who, in their right mind, would ever leave a man like Liam Miller? He had earned his nickname around Duke's hospital as the Heart Whisperer for his incredible skill as a cardiothoracic surgeon, but it was equally fitting for the fact that colleagues, patients and relatives alike all fell head over heels for him.

Practically the whole single, female contingent of the place had wanted to be the one woman to catch Liam's eye. The one woman who could reach the distant and seemingly lonely surgeon. The one woman who could heal his apparently damaged soul.

The fact that he'd never dated any of them had only made Liam all the more coveted. It was one of the first things she'd learned from her fellow scrub nurses the moment she'd arrived at Duke's.

The last thing she'd expected, then, had been for Liam to apparently break all his own rules when he'd asked her out on a date.

And then another.

She'd felt special. And perhaps she'd let that fact go to her head because she'd fallen in love with him, hard and fast. Moreover, she'd been foolish enough—naïve enough—to let herself believe he actually loved her too. That she had, actually, healed him. That was how much of a fool she'd been.

Which was why, when her father had called her with the dreadful news, that last day at Duke's, she'd known that moving away from North Carolina—away from Liam—was the healthiest move all round.

Yet even though, deep down, she'd understood the logic, it had nonetheless been the most torturous and agonising decision of her life. Especially for a girl who'd once believed in happily-ever-afters, and soulmates, and love conquering all.

But she was no longer that young, naïve kid. Liam had taught her that real life wasn't like that, and the simple truth had been that her love—she herself—hadn't been enough. Not for Liam, anyway.

Tilting her head back and jerking her chin out a fraction, Talia summoned a glare of her own.

'I don't play games. I never did.'

But, Lord, it was hard when he looked more

beautiful, more dangerous than ever. So arresting that she was sure her perfidious heart stuttered and stumbled in her chest.

'I used to think that,' he stated flatly. 'Just as I used to think that I knew you.'

Never mind the icy rivers that his dispassionate tone sent coursing through her, it was the way he looked straight through her that sheared off an entire glacier inside her, sending it—and almost her—crashing down to stain the highly polished, ultra-hygienic, stunning marble floor of the painfully opulent, intimidatingly high-tech Island Clinic.

She wanted to rail and argue. But what would be the point?

'It turns out that I never really knew you at all, did I?' Liam added, his acerbic smile so biting she could almost taste the sharp, unpleasant tang of it for herself.

The same bitterness she'd tasted when she'd finally realised that the future she had begun to imagine—one that included Duke's, and Liam— was definitely not the same future he'd envisaged in his own mind. And it never would be.

He might have cared for her, in his odd strange way, but she still hadn't been *enough*.

There was a part of Liam that he had always kept locked away, not just from her but from the world. He'd never truly let her close to him—he'd never let her *in*. If anything, he'd once condemned everything she believed in—love, marriage, family—as whimsical fantasies that had no place in the real world and would never for him.

And, still, the warning signs hadn't been enough to allow her to cut her losses and run. She'd been tied to him. Loving him. Hoping that would be enough to encourage him to open up to her.

Not, of course, that she had expected a man she'd only been dating for a few months to declare undying love and propose marriage and a family. But, equally, she hadn't expected such a man to wreck her in more ways than she'd ever thought possible. Leaving the way she had done had been the only way she'd known to save them both.

And now he was here on her small Caribbean island, and Talia found herself desperately fighting the *maybes,* and the *what-ifs.* As if there was room for such thoughts. But Liam would only be here for a month while he tended to his patient— the kid of one of Hollywood's current brightest stars—and then he would be gone.

She'd be damned if she opened her heart up only to let him wreck her again. She simply couldn't afford to let him see how easily he got under her skin.

How easily he could unravel her.

'I could say the same thing,' she ground out

instead. 'But, really, what would be the point of such a conversation?'

'What indeed?'

His dispassion sliced through her all over again. Leaving her with frost that seemed to spread from the inside out, and had nothing to do with the state-of-the-art air-con of The Island Clinic.

People had warned her that she would end up getting hurt. That Liam Miller was a brilliant surgeon but a lone wolf. A good man but a man with walls. She hadn't believed any of them.

She'd been wrong. Terribly, desperately wrong. But hadn't she already shown Liam enough weakness back then? She'd be damned if she gave him a new demonstration now.

'Is that the reason you sought me out, then? To tell me that you never knew me at all? And to tell me that I was the last person you ever expected to see again? Because I can assure you that I didn't expect to see you either.'

For a moment he didn't answer, he merely smiled. An edgy little quirk of his lips that was so sharp it made Talia itch to check that he hadn't actually cut her. And then he took a step towards her.

Just a single step, and Talia felt as though the entire clinic had lifted and tilted. It was a fight just to stay upright, such was the devastating impact Liam Miller had on her.

Had always had on her, from the moment they'd met on her first day at Duke's.

'I've just met your chief here, at this clinic of yours. He's quite inspiring.'

'Nate?' She grasped the apparently safe topic with both hands. 'Yes, he is. He set up The Island Clinic *and* the sister programme with St Vic's Hospital after the hurricane here a few years ago.'

'I'm well aware of the programme.' His smile became all the more sardonic. 'And I know many surgeons who would cut a limb off themselves with their own scalpel for a chance to work at the famous Island Clinic.'

'Right. Of course.'

He'd taken another step towards her and Talia found she was twisting herself up in knots not to react. Not to show any sign of feeling intimidated.

*Intimidation?* a sly voice asked. *Or attraction?*

'Which made it particularly interesting when the same Nate Edwards contacted me a week ago, asking me if I would like to take a look at a special case.'

Uncertainty coursed through her. His tone was so loaded that she almost thought he knew the truth. But how could he? Nate wouldn't have betrayed her confidence. And now that she'd already pretended not to know what he was doing on the island, she had no choice but to keep feigning innocence.

Still, she flicked a nervous tongue out over suddenly parched lips as she adopted a look of vague interest.

'Oh?'

'*Oh*?' he echoed, a little too breezily for Talia's liking.

An almost dangerous nonchalance. Which was odd if she thought about it as Liam was renowned for his cool, even temperament. So laid-back that it almost dipped into emotional detachment.

Even with her. Which was the part she'd hated the most.

There had been a few moments over the long summer they'd enjoyed together—the briefest of flashes when she'd thought he was about to let his guard down and talk to her. But then the shutters had slammed down abruptly on her again, and she'd been left out in the cold. All his thoughts and feelings his, and his alone.

'So, to be clear, you knew nothing about my arrival?' he challenged, so close now that she had to tilt her neck up to look into his face.

And suddenly she couldn't pretend any more. The electricity practically crackled in the space between them, leaving her feeling shaky and drained. Like she was coiled so tightly inside that she was at risk of jumping out of her own skin at any moment.

Whatever she'd told herself, it seemed her body

was only too willing to undermine it. Even after all this time, it still wanted him. *Ached* for him.

'I knew nothing,' she confirmed, her voice sounding like that of a stranger. 'Obviously, I knew a surgeon was coming in to fill in for Isak on the trial, but I didn't know it was you.'

His eyes bored into her that little bit deeper, causing her entire body to begin to heat. She told herself it was because she hated fibbing. It was why she usually prided herself on never doing so.

'Is that so?' He lifted a hand and, if she hadn't known better, she might have thought he was about to put a stray curl around her ear or caress her cheek.

Obviously, he did neither.

And still Talia didn't answer. She was getting hotter now and somehow the ground had shifted beneath her feet, leaving her scrambling for some kind of purchase. She couldn't explain it.

'Imagine, then,' Liam continued almost conversationally, 'my thoughts when I asked Nate where he'd heard about my work, only for him to inform me that he'd looked into my reputation after one of his scrub nurses had recommended me.'

# CHAPTER TWO

'NATE TOLD YOU?' Talia gasped, shock making her forget her little foray into acting—which was probably for the best since she appeared to be terrible at it.

But why would Nate have done that when she'd asked him not to mention her at all to Liam?

'What did you expect, Talia?' Liam asked evenly. 'He's founder and Chief of Staff of a world-renowned facility, not some kids' playground leader. He wanted to be sure that there was no bad blood between us. Presumably that we would be able to work together.'

Her mouth felt parched. Like a scorched area of forest in the dry season.

'What did you tell him?'

'What do you think I told him?' demanded Liam quietly. Too quietly. 'I explained that while there was an intimate history between us, it was long buried. Then I told him that, whatever our past personal connection, you were one of the most professional scrub nurses that I knew, and that I would be more than happy to work with you again.'

'Oh,' she managed tightly. 'And is that…is that how you feel?'

It didn't help that Liam was eyeing her in such a way that it made her skin feel as though it was too tight for her own body.

'Honestly?' His voice was harsh, and she hated the rush of hope that it sent through her. As though the fact that he wasn't entirely at ease might mean something. 'I'd hoped to come here, perform my surgery, and leave. I didn't consider seeing you. I didn't even know you'd come back here.'

'This is my home,' she blurted out, shocked. 'Where else would I have gone when I left Duke's?'

The silence was all too heavy. All too suffocating. It swirled around them, but eventually it was Liam who spoke.

'I neither knew nor cared.'

A wiser woman would have quit now. But Talia feared she'd never been wise where this man had been concerned. And as much as she hated herself for her weakness, and her desperation, she heard herself answering all the same.

'I think you made that obvious at the time.'

'Is that so?'

She didn't know who had inched that fraction nearer. Bringing them so close to each other that she could feel his warm breath brushing over her cheek. And she wanted…*more*. For one crazy moment she almost imagined what it would be like to lean up and press her lips to his.

If it would feel the same.

'I know you came here for the case. I never thought you would come here for me. If you'd wanted to do that, you'd have done it three years ago.'

The words were out before she could swallow them back.

But, boy, did she wish that she could. She didn't even know where it had come from, or that's what she wanted to tell herself. The worst of it was the way his expression changed instantly from that sharp smile to a look of…almost pure contempt.

Yet oddly, whether it was more at her or himself, she couldn't quite be sure.

'Is that what this is all about—some pathetic test?' he demanded. 'I didn't go racing after you three years ago, but you've finally found a way to get me here now?'

'No,' she cried, horrified. 'Of course not.'

Though it unsteadied her to realise that a tiny part of her wondered if that was exactly what she'd done. She shook her head to dislodge that thought.

'This is exactly why I didn't want Nate to tell you that I'd been the one to recommend you. It isn't about me, or you, it's about a kid who is terrified and has been told by three top surgeons already that her only chance is to get on this trial. And I happened to know that you have performed multiple successful full aortic reconstructions using the RAT approach.'

At least that much was true—he had been successful with several right-anterior thoracotomies—whatever else she might not have realised had been bubbling away in her subconscious.

For several long moments they stood, facing off against each other, and Talia tried to stop herself from visibly shaking.

'I wasn't trying to engineer some ill-fated reunion,' she managed when she couldn't stand the silence any longer. 'Trust me, you're the last person I want to see again, too.'

And it was only as the words came out of her mouth—a touch too melodramatically, if she was being honest with herself—that she realised them for the lie they were.

Ten minutes ago she might have truly believed that she was over Liam but right here, with him standing inches from her, she finally admitted it for the lie that it was.

Liam, however, didn't even blink.

'Funny thing is, I don't believe you.'

'Well, you should. I even asked Nate to take me off surgeries here at the clinic while you were here. In two days I'm scheduled to start a month-long rotation at St Vic's, across the other side of the island.'

'St Vic's?'

She cranked up her smile once more and told herself that his icy tone didn't hurt. Not at all.

'St Vic's is the local hospital about fifteen miles outside our capital, Williamtown. It isn't a patch on The Island Clinic, of course, but Nate's main aim in setting up the clinic was to enable it to fund new equipment for St Vic's, and for the local community to also have some access to the world-class medical team of the clinic, via an outreach programme.'

'Yes, thank you for the tour-guide spiel but I'm well informed on the history between St Vic's Hospital and The Island Clinic.' His tone was clipped. 'My surprise was more about the fact that you apparently didn't want your chief of staff to know there was any problem between us, yet you asked to be transferred while I was here.'

'Oh.'

She shifted awkwardly and his nostrils flared slightly. Once upon a time it had meant that he wanted her. Now she could only imagine it meant he was resenting the amount of time he was letting her take up.

'I assure you, Liam,' she pressed on hastily, 'if you hadn't arrived here today—two days earlier than planned, I should point out—we wouldn't have seen each other at all.'

Something swept through those green eyes of his and, not for the first time, she wished to God that she could read whatever was going on in this beautiful, enigmatic man's head.

If she'd been able to years ago, surely it would have spared her a mess of heartache? It was almost impossible to remember now how she'd once believed that nothing could ever have made her walk away from someone as incredible as Liam. Or how her love for him had turned, so quickly, to such pain.

'You really didn't expect us to see each other at all whilst I was working on this case?' he demanded curtly, after what felt like an eternity.

Her head was a leaden weight as she bobbed it once in assent. The air pressed in around them, almost suffocating, and she wished it didn't hurt half as much as it did.

'I recommended you when Isak had his boating accident, simply because I knew you were the best chance of a successful procedure for Lucy.' And if there was a little voice in her head calling her out for being a liar, she would be damned if she acknowledged it.

'Why me?'

'Because I know Nate. For him, finding a replacement cardiothoracic surgeon wasn't just about finding one who was at the top of his game—although that's a given, of course—it's also about finding someone who would be the right fit for his team.'

'And you decided that was me? Even meaning we would have to work together?'

'I knew you would fit in. And I was right,' she pressed on, needing to say the words. 'You said you know of Nate Edwards so you must know that The Island Clinic, and its vulnerable patients, are all that ever matters to him.'

'That and the local hospital.' Liam jerked his head in assent. 'I heard that he set the clinic up following a hurricane here, as a way to fund St Vic's Hospital and help the locals.'

It was hell. standing here almost toe to toe with Liam and refusing to let herself back away.

Hell. And heaven.

Only in those late-night dreams, which she'd pretended she didn't really have, had she imagined the two of them ever being this close again.

'Right,' she managed hoarsely. 'But even though The Island Clinic is renowned for its A-list patient base—from the NFL to Hollywood, and from Aruba to the USA—he also ensures locals have full use of the facilities if they need it.'

'I thought the clinic was known as a place for the elite, where they could be assured of utter discretion as they benefited from the absolute gold standard of medical care, with the best medical professionals?'

'It is,' she confirmed. Could he hear her heart thundering on her chest wall? To her, the sound was almost deafening. 'It's a place where A-listers like Violet Silnag-Wells come, whose daughter, Lucy, is your new patient and who needs a full atrial arch reconstruction. But Nate also uses the helicopter pad to fly locals here if St Vic's can't meet their needs. He really cares about patients in both the clinic, and St Vic's Hospital. Every single one of them matters to him and I knew that was something you, of all people, would understand.'

Liam jerked back. She actually saw the minute movement as he moved away from her. As though he hadn't been expecting her to say anything like that. To compliment him.

Instinctively, Talia pressed home whatever advantage she might have.

'It was no wonder Nate practically bit my arm off after I told him about Duke's rising star, Heart Whisperer. But for the record, Liam. I'm not on the trial team. I never was. So this couldn't possibly have been about you and me working together again.

'It only later occurred to me that if you came here, we might end up face to face,' she choked out. At least, that was the story she was sticking to. Even in her own mind. 'Which is why I asked for a month-long transfer. I thought that if I was at the hospital, it would be better all round.'

For one long moment neither of them spoke. And then, abruptly, Liam took a step backwards.

And even though there was no reason on earth for that to make her feel it like a loss, Talia felt bereft.

'Fine,' he ground out, his tone a mixture of irritation, displeasure and something else she couldn't put her finger on. 'That's a solution I can live with.'

Then, before she could even formulate the words for any kind of response, he was gone. His shoes echoed down the corridor, haunting her long after he'd disappeared from view.

*What the hell was the matter with him?* Liam berated himself furiously as he stalked through the indecently opulent corridors of The Island Clinic. This was his penance for searching her out. Yet what choice had he had? He'd been drawn to seek her out the moment Nate had confirmed that Talia had been the one to recommend him.

Fury, and something else he didn't care to identify, pounded inside him. It thumped along every inch of his skin, bubbling and exploding in his veins, and making him…*feel* things that he had precisely zero interest in feeling. As though he had no control whatsoever of his own body.

*He,* who prided himself on never letting anything, any*one,* rile him. *Ever.*

Yet if he hadn't walked out of that room at that moment, he feared he wouldn't have been able to stop himself from hauling Talia into his arms and taking that one last truth that existed between them to use it to show her up for the liar that she was.

Because whatever other tales and falsehoods had ever fallen from her mouth—including the lie that she hadn't even realised he was coming to St Victoria—there was one area in which she had never been able to deceive him.

That attraction which had always fizzed and arced between them was no fabrication. It never had been. Perhaps it was the only real thing the two of them had ever shared, but that didn't make it any less effective.

He'd read it in every line of that sensual body of hers. Every shallow breath. Every darkened regard. Whatever else she might want to pretend, she couldn't fake disinterest in him.

And what perturbed Liam the most…was that neither could he.

He could tell himself that he was shocked at seeing Talia again. He could claim that it was seething rage that drummed through his body. But, deep down, he knew it was something far more potent than anger.

It was desire. And it galled him beyond all measure to have to admit it.

He wanted her just as he had always wanted her; from the very first moment he'd laid eyes on her with her bubbling laughter and killer body. Sex—incredible sex—had never been one of their failings. Quite the opposite, in fact. The sex had always been intense. Exceptional.

Then on top of that his attraction to her had swollen tenfold when he'd seen how focussed and skilled she was in the operating room.

The whole package.

But there were some things more intimate than sex even. And if he'd ever stood a chance of opening up to any woman on a more intimate level he'd considered that maybe it would have been with Talia.

Instead, she'd left. Without a word.

Which was all the more reason why he had to stay cool and detached. He had to. Because if he didn't—if he'd stayed in that room with her just now—he was terribly doubtful that he could have controlled that…*thing* from heating up between them all over again. Drawing him in. And he wouldn't have realised until it was too late and the flames were licking around him—like the fable of the boiling frog.

And Liam decided that he had no intention of being like any such member of the amphibian family.

He, who was renowned for his cool head and soothing composure under even the most stressful emergencies.

It wasn't just an art he'd honed as a doctor, and a surgeon; it was a skill he'd been perfecting his entire life. A logical defence mechanism given the way his father had always looked on him as an abomination.

From as early as Liam could remember, his curt old man had pounded into him the need to *be* something, *do* something, prove that his life was worth his mother losing hers. An angry, scornful, grief-stricken man who had never been able to get over the death of the one love of his life; or the fact that it had been his infant son who had caused it.

As a child, he had believed every cruel word of it. By the time he'd grown into an adult it had been too late. His own grief and guilt had permanent squatting rights in his chest, like the kind of dark, ugly, twisted twin gargoyles that had adorned the gothic buildings of his childhood boarding school.

He had realised long ago that nothing he could ever do would ever be enough to satisfy his father, or make up for his mother's death. But the need to try had ended up giving him an incredible career and turning him into the rising star surgeon that he was today. So in some perverse way he was grateful for those ruthless lessons.

And if, on a social level, people thought him cold and detached, what had that mattered? He'd accepted that love was never going to feature heavily in it. He didn't trust it when people said it to him, and he certainly wasn't capable of giving it back.

Until Talia.

Even now, something stirred deep down, even further inside him than the blackness of that hollow pit where he pretended the worst of his guilt and shame did not reside.

Kissing her would have been a miscalculation of gargantuan proportions.

Because the truth was that he had never felt more rattled, his thoughts charging around his head like some trapped wild animal—desperate to break out. But wasn't that the way Talia had always made him feel?

As though his entire life—until her arrival—had been a cage. And she had been the key to unlocking it and finally setting him free.

Now, though, his body felt so tense and coiled that he might as well have gone several rounds in a ring, even though he hadn't boxed since boarding school, and certainly not from the moment he'd realised he'd wanted to become a surgeon.

He felt as though he needed to break out of his own skin.

Having managed to navigate the identical marble corridors back to the indecently opulent consultation room that Nate had just allocated to him, Liam strode inside. Every inch of this place oozed money. A place designed for the celebrity elite. It was such a far cry from the way the rest of the island lived; no wonder Nate had set up the foundation, using the income generated by The

Island Clinic to fund an outreach programme to provide better care to the rest of the community.

He reached behind him and closed the door firmly, letting his hand rest there just a little longer. As if satisfying himself that the piece of furniture was closed enough to also shut out the deluge of memories that had threatened to crash over him ever since he'd stood in that doorway and seen Talia inside.

Of course it didn't work—the images swept in all the same. Those vibrant colours were everywhere, and their songs of exuberance, and joy, and vitality were as resonant as ever.

He threw himself down into his ridiculously luxurious chair, his too-long legs stretched out in front of him, disgusted with himself, and angrily schooling his thoughts.

Contempt flooded through him. He was insane, acting like some kind of hormone-ravaged adolescent. He hadn't come here for a woman. He had barely even remembered that Talia had once told him she originally hailed from this glorious island of St Victoria.

*Liar,* a voice said in his head.

He ignored that, too, instead reminding that snide internal voice that the only reason he was here was because any case at The Island Clinic was a good career opportunity for him. The next step in his bright career. In his future.

Talia Johnson was his past. He'd barely pieced

himself back together after she'd left him, Liam thought as he staunchly ignored the pounding that now felt as though it was about to burst its way through his skin.

*So the past was exactly where she needed to stay.*

# CHAPTER THREE

THE KNOCK ON his door came much sooner than he'd anticipated. Though he immediately recognised that he *had* anticipated it.

What he hadn't expected was for the door to open and for Talia to step inside before he could even answer.

'I believe it's customary to wait for the person inside to answer.' He raised his eyebrows, but at least his voice felt more even now. More controlled.

The way it should be.

He just had to remember that coming to The Island Clinic was about a case, a career opportunity—whatever this sorceress of a woman said by way of atonement.

Talia, however, didn't appear in the least bit apologetic. Instead, she kept coming at him boldly.

'I might have waited,' she threw at him, 'if I hadn't thought you'd leave me waiting out there all day.'

It galled that a part of him still admired her characteristic spirit. It was one of the things that had attracted him in the first place—her feistiness, her humour, her intelligence.

*And that damned killer body.*

Liam despaired of himself as another familiar punch of attraction slammed into him, dragging his gaze across the room and tempting him. The very danger he'd anticipated—and, still, he succumbed. His eyes took in every inch of her—the way he hadn't had a chance to do earlier when he'd been so close to her. When he hadn't been able to resist that magnetic pull between them.

Her eyes were still like the deepest, richest pools of warm chocolate, those dimples still dancing in her cheeks when she talked, the line of her neck as elegant as he remembered. Her hair was tied up in that professional bun she always wore, but he suspected that if he went over and pulled it free, it would be the same glossy black curls that tumbled, wild and magnificent, just past her shoulders. Fierce and charismatic, just like Talia herself.

And then his gaze dropped lower to those generous breasts, which had always spilled so gloriously over his hands; the sweet nip of her waist and then the delectable flare of her hips. He could swear he remembered every indentation and every curve, and his mouth practically watered.

'For someone who has just assured me that we won't be seeing anything of each other at all while I'm at The Island Clinic, I have to say I'm surprised that you followed me.'

She bristled, and he considered it was amazing how he could inject such a note of insouciance into his tone when his chest now felt as though it was so tight that he was struggling to breathe evenly.

Still, she lifted her head.

'I feel I ought to apologise.'

'Is that so?'

Was it so wrong of him to relish the way she blinked then, as if she couldn't quite work him out? Good, let her realise he wasn't the same easy mark he'd been last time they'd met.

'I…shouldn't have fibbed to you about being the one to recommend you to Nate.'

Liam couldn't drag his eyes away. Especially when she seemed to stiffen slightly as his gaze moved over her, then shifted. A slight movement that made him think, with altogether too much clarity, of the way she'd used to move in his arms. When he'd touched her with his hands and then the way she'd arched when he'd replaced them with his mouth. If he listened closely, Liam was positive he could hear echoes of the way she'd screamed his name as he'd pitched her over the edge and into the brilliant flames.

And he abhorred himself for such weakness. He needed to get a grip. *Now*.

'So why did you?' he demanded. 'Recommend me, that is?'

She wrinkled her nose, as if she was finding

the conversation even harder than he was. He didn't care to identify why he found that so gratifying.

'What do you want me to say, Liam? You already know that Nate needed someone who was not only experienced in total atrial arch reconstruction, and in the right anterior mini-thoracotomy, but who would also be an acceptable replacement for Isak to carry on the trial.'

'And you thought of me over anyone else.'

Another nose-wrinkle. He used to know it to mean she was holding something back. Now he wasn't so sure he knew what anything she did really meant.

'I did, Liam, because the trial that Isak was doing is ground-breaking. In precisely the area in which you excel.'

He did not feel flattered. He *would* not feel flattered. He did not feel that unwelcome fist, which pulled tight and rough around his chest. For a man who was renowned for always being self-possessed and confident, no matter what the circumstances, right now he felt about as far from composed as it was possible to be.

Yet as Talia talked he felt some of the heat, the shock of earlier begin to dissipate. He could cope with this professional conversation far more easily than he could handle the personal one. And it was surprising how easily they were falling back into easy conversation now the topic was…safer.

'There have been plenty of studies out there comparing different approaches, including MS, PUH and RAT,' he pointed out. 'They've looked at everything from intubation times to transfusions, surgical revision for bleeding to wound infection, length of ICU stay before in-hospital death, and still the list goes on and on. What makes this one so different?'

She didn't even hesitate.

'Those other studies have compared the three approaches when the right-anterior thoracotamy was a relatively new approach, so surgeons were still on a steep learning curve. It stands to reason that it's taken time to hone the technique, but now experienced surgeons, like you and Isak, have significantly reduced timings such as cross-clamp times, and cardiopulmonary bypass times, resulting in the patient being on the table for up to half an hour less. On top of that...'

'Fine.' He raised his hand to stop her. 'You've made your point.'

She'd always been a great scrub nurse, passionate and knowledgeable, as she'd just proved. Yet she'd claimed not to be on the previous surgeon's team. He couldn't help but wonder why.

'I didn't realise I was making a point, merely answering your question,' she levelled at him. 'Hopefully I've now proved to you that I recommended you to Nate for entirely appropriate reasons and not to...to lure you St Victoria.'

'I didn't say you had.'

'You implied it.' She shrugged.

He didn't bother denying it.

The fact was she had presented a coherent explanation—precisely as he'd challenged her to do. So why didn't he feel entirely satisfied?

Instead, he felt strangely flat, as if a part of him had hoped there *had* been some personal motivation behind it all.

How was it that this one woman always managed to sneak under his skin, when no one else ever had?

It irked. Yet still something had thrummed in his chest. Something he might have thought to be suspiciously like a heart—if he hadn't known it to be impossible. As if he was *glad* she was back in his life.

Liam shoved the thought aside angrily.

For his own sake, he should leave. Get as far away from St Victoria—and Talia Johnson—as possible. Hadn't he learned his lesson with her last time? There was only person in life that anyone could trust—and that was themselves. Everyone else would always let you down in the end.

But this wasn't all about Talia any more. He was committed to The Island Clinic now. To Nate Edwards. There was a patient flying in for his expertise and, no matter the personal cost, he prided himself on his professionalism. He wouldn't let them down.

'I accept your apology,' he rasped out at last.

'My apology?'

'That you shouldn't have lied about being the one to recommend me to your chief.'

'I didn't apologise, I just said—'

'However, I'm satisfied that you recommended me for professional reasons rather than personal.' He knew he sounded stilted, wooden, but he couldn't seem to help himself.

'Oh. Good. That's great.' Her breath came out in a rush, and if she'd noticed how awkward he'd sounded she wasn't mentioning it.

'Good.'

There was a beat of silence as they remained immobile, eying each other cautiously.

Then another beat.

Furious with himself again, Liam gave himself a mental shake.

'Right, well, if that's it, I have some work to do,' he gritted out.

'Of course.' She spun around quickly, almost stumbling, and he was halfway out of his seat before he realised what he was doing. He was still reacting to her even though she had made it abundantly clear that she was wholly indifferent to him.

He dropped back again and stretched his legs back out so that Talia didn't realise it, too.

But it wasn't enough. He couldn't stop himself,

he wanted to affect her the way she affected him. To hurt her, even in some small way.

'I take it your plan is still to work in the other hospital on this island for the duration of my stay?'

She turned haltingly.

'I thought it would be a solution you would prefer.'

'That would suggest I cared one way or another about what you do.' He forced himself to sound detached.

'So...you're happy for me to stay at The Island Clinic?'

Clearly, she loved her job here, just as he'd suspected.

'You misunderstand,' he rasped out. 'I'm not interested in where you work, just as long as you aren't working on my case. Do we have an understanding?'

She flicked her tongue over her lips, suggesting new nervousness, though he couldn't read the expression on her lovely face. But then he told himself that he didn't want to.

'Yes, okay.' She dipped her head once. 'We have an understanding.'

And then she turned again, closed her fingers around the door handle and began yanking it open as if she couldn't wait to get out of there.

Which suited him just fine.

Talia was halfway to stalking out of the room

and into the corridor before her newfound meekness began to disappear, eroded by the temper that people rarely saw but never forgot.

Liam had never seen that temper. But, then, she'd never seen this side of him either, so she supposed that made them even.

She'd always known he was authoritative. A strong, confident surgeon who ran his operating room precisely how he liked to. But *this* Liam—the one who seemed just a little less self-restrained, as if something was bubbling terribly close to the surface—was a different entity entirely. As if their unscheduled reunion had unsettled him just as much as it had her.

And Talia found she rather liked it—the idea that she was seeing another side to this fascinating, infuriating man.

What appealed to her far less, however, was the way he had just dismissed her; waving her away like some kind of irritating mosquito.

Swinging around before she could second-guess herself, Talia marched back across the room to stand in front of his desk, her arms outstretched as she leaned on the table.

'You know, for a man who never wanted to see me again, and whose career trajectory these past few years has pretty much only been matched by that of a space rocket, you seem to be surprisingly bothered by my presence.'

She realised her mistake too late. Her moment

of bravado, striding up to his desk, had brought her altogether too close to Liam.

As he jerked up to his feet, the movement brought him forward until there was barely a few inches between them.

*Again.*

Close enough to touch him.

Her heart kicked hard. She clutched harder at the edge of the table in an effort to keep her hands in check. *Lord help her but if she leaned forward, she could kiss him.* She might have resisted insane impulses once, but she wasn't sure she had the strength to do it again.

'I have to say, Talia, I always knew you had passion—I admired it, in fact—but I don't recall you being this vehement.'

'Perhaps I wasn't quite as much myself with you as I always thought I was.' The words spilled out of her mouth before she'd even thought them in her head.

Liam frowned, clearly not liking that. She didn't know whether that was a good thing or a bad one.

'Which means what? Precisely?'

Talia didn't answer. Was this really the conversation she'd wanted to have?

'Please, don't stop now.' He arched an eyebrow. 'A moment ago you clearly had something you wanted to say.'

He was goading her, and that stab of ire flashed though her again.

'All right,' she bit out. 'I think perhaps these past few years have given me a little more clarity, and I've realised a few things.'

'Indeed?'

'Yes.' She pursed her lips. 'I wonder if I was ever entirely myself around you, Liam.'

'And by that you mean?' He clearly didn't like what she was saying.

His expression told her as much.

'I mean that, as much as I've hated to admit it, I think I was a little in awe of everything back in North Carolina. A new hospital, a new country, a new way of life. And then, on top of all that, *you.*'

'Me, on top of all that?' he drawled. 'I'm piqued.'

'That isn't what I meant.' She flushed, instantly trying to shut down the memory, but she was too slow.

Heat spread through her, intense and decalescent, as she recalled just how Liam had made her come apart with the faintest touch of his hand— or his tongue. She wondered if he was thinking the same. How he had made her plead, and sob, and scream until she'd been drained and exhausted, sprawled in his arms and still wanting more.

Always wanting more. Little wonder that she'd believed herself to have been in love.

Now she wondered if she'd allowed herself to be swept up in the sheer Cinderella nature of their relationship, without ever admitting that she'd been slightly intimidated by him.

'Your body tells me different,' he ground out, and she felt a wallop of something entirely inappropriate as he leaned over the other side of the desk.

She was powerless to drag her gaze from his physique, once more on display.

*What was the matter with her?*

Tick.

She could actually hear the clock on the wall above her head, and still neither of them moved. Or spoke.

Tock.

His brows knitted together tightly in a way that was so agonisingly familiar that Talia—despairing of herself—had to clutch the desk white-knuckle-tight in an effort not to reach out and smooth it out.

Tick.

Desperation lent her another burst of daring—or maybe it was foolhardiness. Who knew?

'And what if it did?' she demanded hotly. 'You made it clear you weren't interested in me.'

'I didn't say anything of the sort.'

His voice grazed through her, like a blade that scraped at her and made her raw. Only somehow it was more stimulating than agonising.

She tried to speak but the words stuck in her throat.

'You said—'

'I said that I hadn't ever expected—or hoped—to see you again,' he rasped. 'Not that I wasn't interested.'

Talia was aware that he was advancing on her but she couldn't seem to make herself move. She shook her head wordlessly, unsure if it was the uncharacteristic, dangerous edge to his tone or his sheer, dizzying proximity that was sending her head into a spin. More likely it was the three years' worth of feelings she'd thought long dealt with but which, it was now turning out, had only barely been repressed.

'You still want me?' she managed at last.

Whole lifetimes might have passed, or maybe it was instantaneous, but suddenly his hands were deliciously on her shoulders, as big and strong as she remembered, and his face right next to hers. Eyes that were simultaneously black with desire and hot shimmered in front of her, making her feel...*everything*.

'Against everything my head is telling me,' he growled. 'I came here for my patient, not for you. Yet here you are, haunting me like some kind of spectre.'

Abruptly, like some flip of a switch, he seemed to stop fighting and his mouth came down on hers, as if staking his claim after too many years apart—possessing her. Like leaping headlong into a volcano just as it was erupting.

He kissed her long, and thoroughly, and expertly, as only Liam had ever done to her. A kiss that was simultaneously a punishment and a gift.

His hands held her head just as he wanted it, taking the kiss deeper and deeper. Lazy, drugging kisses that were more and more perfect with every delicious stroke of his tongue, leaving her feeling high and as though she was bouncing off the walls.

'So what is this?' she muttered almost feverishly, when they finally came up for air, barely able to tear her mouth from his for fear that he wouldn't let her back again afterwards. 'Some grand reunion between two old lovers?'

'No reunion,' he rumbled ruthlessly, his voice all silk and menace as the words rasped against her lips and reverberated straight down to between her legs. 'Try more like a long-overdue exorcism.'

# CHAPTER FOUR

THE WORDS SHOULD have pulled her up sharply, but Talia was already too far gone to react.

She was heat and need and fire. Scorched through. It felt as though she was about to burn alive, caught in a blaze that was as thorough as it was devastating. And she revelled in every single second of it.

It was as if this, Liam, now, was all that existed, and none of the other stuff even mattered. As if they could stay like this all day. All week.

For ever.

*But they can't,* yelled a faint voice. It was muffled, indistinct, as though buried under thousands of tons of glowing magma, but it was there all the same. Prodding her with all the things she wanted to forget, especially right at this moment. Reminding her that a world existed outside this dangerously temporary, recklessly seductive little bubble.

She lifted her hands to his chest, telling herself that she needed to push him away. But somehow her arms couldn't quite summon the strength. Instead, she found herself defiantly gripping his lapels and obstinately pulling him closer. And Liam seemed only too willing to comply.

His kisses changed. Less volcanic now, taking on an almost lazy rhythm as his tongue dipped in and out of her mouth, sampling, teasing, and leaving her aching for more.

She could hear the soft little greedy sounds coming from her own throat, but she was helpless to stop herself. This was so much like before, in North Carolina…only not. He took his time, indulging and demanding. His tongue teased hers, slick and hot, before his teeth grazed her lips, making her crave more. Over and over, like they had all the time in the world.

And Talia didn't know whether it was the separation, or that she was older, or a change of perspective, but however intense and glorious it had ever been with Liam three years ago, it felt like a pale imitation of whatever seared between them now.

It was as though time had heightened all those sensations, magnified all those emotions, instead of diminishing them, like it was supposed to have done.

His hands felt molten hot and a slick lava flow eased magnificently over every inch of her body, making her long to tear away the fabric barrier between them. Liam's eyes held hers so darkly, fixedly. As though he could read those wanton thoughts. As though nothing else mattered. As though she was the only thing in this world for him at this moment.

He moulded her to him and once again every inch of them pressed against each other, and she shivered as she felt her softness press against the hardest part of him. When all the words and emotions were stripped out, it all came down to this, didn't it? Man's most primitive, licentious desire.

And the physical side of their relationship had never been a concern, had it? She'd lost count of the number of blissful times they had merged so closely—so carnally—that they hadn't known where one of them had ended and the other begun.

It was only the emotional side of things that had been all barriers and barbs.

She didn't know how she found the strength to lift her head and bring her eyes back to his. But when she did, the air left her lungs with a whoosh. His eyes were dark, wanton, the message in them clear and unmistakable, and calling right down to the depths of her very soul. And he was still staring at her as though she was the most precious thing in the entire world.

*But you aren't*, screamed that same faint voice, and even though she wanted to pretend otherwise, Talia knew what was happening was sheer madness. Nothing had changed between them and deep down a part of her knew that. And still she couldn't tear herself away, she couldn't stop this inexorable pull to him. More to the point, she didn't want to.

His tongue slid rapturously against hers as he kissed her over and over. He cupped her cheeks, angling her head for a better fit.

She was caught in the devastating flow that was rolling over them both, a slow swell of memories that melded the past and the present, making the moment all the more delicious. And even though she knew she shouldn't—even though she knew the sanest thing would be to stop this madness and walk away—she couldn't. She wanted more. So much more.

Before she could second-guess herself, Talia ran her hands over his chest, forcing herself to slow down and savour the moment. It was impossible to stop herself from trembling. His sculpted abs were unmistakable under the thin fabric, their feel so painfully familiar.

How many times had they danced this tango? Toppling through the door of his apartment, often not even able to make it to bedroom before his hands were on her. His mouth. His tongue. And she'd welcomed him—more than welcomed him—she'd ached for him. Coming apart over and over, before pressing him down to the bed and straddling him, while he'd let her take control.

Had she ever been foolish enough to think that

the power had really been hers, though? Liam had always been the one to wield it, hadn't he?

She had always lost her head where Liam was concerned, turning her back on everything else, even her own family. Her old life. Staying in North Carolina in the vain hope that he would begin to feel about her even a fraction of the emotions that she felt—*had* felt—for him.

But they weren't in North Carolina now, were they? They were *here*. In St Victoria. *Her* home. And they'd already agreed that whatever happened over the next month meant nothing. It was about the physical, not the emotional. This magic that had always existed between them and which, no matter what else had gone so inevitably wrong in their relationship, had always been so very perfect in and of itself.

And the truth was that she'd lost something infinitely more precious than her head. She'd lost her heart. So really, she thought dizzily, was it any wonder that when he gathered her in his arms and moved them both around until her bottom was perched on the edge of his desk, she didn't resist. Or when her wrists were encircled by one of his hands, pinning them up against his chest.

If she'd wanted to pull herself free, she could have. It was therefore telling that she did exactly as Liam silently commanded.

And then he began to trace his way down her

body, taking in every dip and every curve, as if relearning them, for the first time in three years.

Talia couldn't have said exactly what it was that rolled through her at that moment. A kind of bitter-sweet regret, perhaps, which stole the breath from her lungs. She only knew she wanted this moment to go on for ever, even as she despaired of herself for her weakness.

The way she melted as he slid his hands up and down her sides, inching their way until they were cupping her too-heavy breasts and then, after what felt like an eternity, raking his thumb pads over her achingly sensitive nipples.

Even through her scrubs, the effect was electric, evidenced by the involuntary, raw sound that was wrenched from her throat.

'All in good time,' Liam muttered immediately.

Gratifyingly, his voice was nowhere near as composed as she thought he might have liked. There was comfort to be taken from that, at least.

But then she couldn't think any more because he was trailing his hands lower. Down her sides, and around to the small hollow at the base of her spine. Caressing and re-educating himself like she was a new, fascinating subject in which he wished to school himself.

And then he was sliding his fingers under the hem of her top. Inching under so that they skimmed her bare waist, making her entire body contract with desire. Dear God, if he made her this edgy from mere caresses, what might happen if he did more?

She couldn't manage more than a whisper, though she could hear her deep breaths loud and clear.

'Liam…'

She ought to remind him where they were…if only her mind wasn't a dim fug of nothing.

'Like I said, all in good time,' he repeated, his voice scratchy.

And then, as her hooded eyes caught his, she felt his hand dip beneath her waistband, down, lower still, until her throat was too choked to speak, and her body too aroused to object.

He teased her. Taunted her, even. Letting his fingers creep lower as they traced exquisite whorls wherever they went. *Everywhere* they went. Except for where she needed him most.

'I know,' he muttered, as some desperate squeak escaped her. 'Trust me, I understand.'

But if he did, then he wasn't giving in to it. Not quite yet. He wanted to keep her dangling, like a fish on a hook as the fishermen did out there in the deep blue sea.

'Liam,' she managed again.

'Why the rush?' he growled.

'No rush.' Talia had no idea how she managed to answer, though she sounded embarrassingly out of breath. 'I just…'

'You just…?' he echoed mercilessly. 'Just this, perhaps?'

But before she could reply, he dipped his fingers lower, dragging through her hair and sending devilish shivers right through her body.

'Or this?'

With another twist of his wrist, he let his fingers abrade her. Right where she was hottest, slickest—where she needed him most.

'Like that, then?' he confirmed, a certain triumph in his tone.

Clearly, he didn't need her to answer. Her body's reactions did all the talking for her.

As he stroked her, flicking his fingers over her, tearing low cries from her with every pass, sensations pummelled her from every direction. So much more than every fantasy she'd had over the last three years. Because there had been no one else for Talia in all that time.

What would have been the point? No one could ever have matched Liam. She wondered if he knew that. If he knew that he was the only person who had ever, *ever* gone where he was now.

'Is this what you want?' he demanded, his tone thicker now.

Talia couldn't answer, it was taking all she had not to cry out. He was stroking her fast now, one hand in her panties, the other cupping her cheek. When had he released her hands? She didn't even know, but now they lay almost flimsily against that granite chest.

He angled his head to kiss her again, his fingers still playing that irresistible rhythm on her body, and she was helpless to resist. Between his mouth and his hand, she was adrift. Floating off on a sea of bliss with every skilful stroke.

He built the tempo quickly—or maybe it was just that she couldn't stop herself. That wild, wanton pace that dragged such low, primal sounds from deep inside her, and made her entire body begin to quiver, pushing herself against his hand as though it could somehow hasten those glorious final moments.

And then, as the edge of that chasm raced ever closer, and her body began to shake and come apart, Talia felt his lips on that sensitive hollow of her throat, and she couldn't fight it any longer.

It was like being hurled into the air. Flying and hurtling, all at once. Not even caring that she was out of control, as long as she kept coming apart, over and over again. She thought he would stop, but he didn't. He just kept going, sending her off in this direction and then that one. Propelling her wherever he wanted her to go.

And she simply gave in to it. As if there was nothing else she could do. As if there was nothing else she *wanted* to be doing.

Finally, she began to fall. Twisting and spinning as she gained more and more momentum.

The ground was racing towards her too fast. Dimly, Talia realised, the best that she could hope for was that Liam would be there, at the bottom, to cushion her fall.

Liam felt her pull away from him, a startled sound on her lips.

Doing something like this in his new place of work should have been the most indecorous thing he'd ever done. Yet watching Talia—his Talia— crack and splinter beneath his touch was too raunchy for him to care about what was proper and what wasn't.

It felt as though he'd been waiting a lifetime for this moment again. And now it was here, he didn't want to let it go.

Talia, however, clearly had different plans.

He stood motionless as she put some distance between them, then adjusted her scrubs with shaky hands. When she stood up again, her eyes blazed at him.

'What the hell was that about?'

'Do I really need to explain it?' he questioned dryly. 'You're a medical professional after all.'

She actually gritted her teeth at him, and it was all he could do not to smile at how adorable she looked.

'I mean, was that your way of proving a point?'

'A point?'

'You thought I recommended you to my chief

of staff to get you here, to St Victoria. Is this your way of proving that was true?'

'I wasn't actually setting out to prove any-thing,' he replied evenly, though the dangerous fact remained that he hadn't been able to think of anything at all. 'All the same, it's a little late to be acting so prudish, don't you think?'

She glowered at him even harder.

'No, I don't think it's too late at all.'

'Really?' he challenged. 'When I only have to do this to taste you?'

And then, to ram the point home, he lifted his hand to his mouth and sucked on his fingers.

She made a half-gurgling sound, and her eyes widened all the more. Liam was grateful for her indignation. At least it meant she was too preoc-cupied to see how affected he was by what was happening between them. How badly he wanted to taste her on his tongue properly.

He really needed to get out of the office and take a moment to regroup.

'I think it was,' she whispered, at last.

Too quietly, for Liam's peace of mind. Too con-trolled. He wanted to find safe ground before he lost what was left of his fragile self-control with Talia but the left and the right side of her brain didn't appear to be on the same page.

'Was what?'

'A test,' she said. 'You wanted to get your re-venge.'

'Revenge for what?' he bit out instantly.

'You more or less accused me of leaving Duke's—*you*—in the way that I did because I wanted to goad you into racing here to St Victoria, after me.' Her voice shook, though he thought it was more out of shame than anger. 'I think this is your way of getting revenge.'

'I'm insulted that you would think so little of me,' he ground out. 'I might think any number of things about what happened three years ago, but what just happened was about primal lust. Revenge didn't come into it for a second.'

However, he had no intention whatsoever of revealing what emotions *had* entered into his decision to blow up every career rule he'd ever had, and do that with Talia. Here. Now.

He could barely even think straight. He might have given Talia her release, but he had denied himself his own. Now his body was making it clear to him exactly how badly it wanted to claim her the way he knew they both wanted. However much they were each trying to deny it.

But these were base desires, and he refused to give in to them. He tried to focus on her words.

'You still want me, but you don't love me,' Talia was hurling at him. 'You told me that you never could.'

'That isn't who I am,' he said curtly.

'Why not, though?' she cried. 'Because your mother died and your father is a bit cold?'

'You're venturing onto thin ice, Talia. I suggest that you think carefully about voicing next whatever is in your head.'

'That's always the problem, though, isn't it?' she challenged. 'Any time things get too personal, you back away.'

'I have never backed away from anything.' He narrowed his eyes, but it hadn't escaped her that he'd hesitated for a split second.

Sucking in a deep breath, she pressed on.

'That's exactly what you do, Liam. Any time we ever veered towards the personal, you found a way to change the conversation.'

'I beg to differ.' His tone was easy, almost scornfully amused. 'You told me all about your parents and your two younger brothers; even how close you are to your grandmother. And, equally, I told you about mine,' he countered before he'd even thought about it.

He only realised he'd said something out of keeping when Talia froze, blinking at him.

'Your grandmother?' she asked. He didn't elaborate, so she pressed on. 'You never once even mentioned her, let alone told me anything about her.'

Had he not? He was sure he had. He'd thought about it, from time to time, anyway. The only other person to have ever shown him affection, aside from Talia. In some respects, his fiery St Victorian woman had resembled his spirited grandmother. Gloria by name, and by character. The only person who had ever stood up to his father and stood up for Liam himself against her only son's hatred of his own child.

But that had been before she, too, had died. Abandoning him once again to a lonely life with the old man.

'I told you about her when I showed you that box I had.'

She tilted her head to one side.

'You showed me a box which you told me contained photos of your mother that you never looked at. But you never once mentioned your grandmother, Liam.'

Had he really never mentioned her to Talia? Even once? He didn't realise that he'd said the words aloud, until Talia responded.

'No. You didn't. You never really told me anything. Did you never ask yourself why I left, Liam? Did you never wonder about anything?'

'I wondered,' he stated simply. 'But if you'd wanted to tell me, you would have.'

'I *did* want to tell you. I didn't feel I could. You actively avoided conversation about your own family. I know because I tried—several times. You shut me out, Liam. You always shut me out.'

'I barely knew you,' he countered. 'Was I to tell you my entire life story?'

He might have known she wouldn't be so easily put off.

'Have you ever told it to anyone? Any part of it?'

Liam didn't answer. He wasn't entirely sure what had happened in the last few moments. His head was swimming and he didn't even know where to start with untangling the knot of conflicting thoughts.

How had this unwanted conversation even begun? If he could go back and stop it, he would. As it was, he needed to find a way to change it. Now.

'This is a pointless conversation.' He barely recognised his own clipped tone. 'It isn't going to get us anywhere.'

'No, you just won't allow it happen.' There was a sadness in her voice that clawed at him.

He thrust it aside.

'I came here for my patient, and for the trial,' he managed coldly.

For a moment he thought she was going to argue something more, but then she lifted her shoulders in the briefest of shrugs.

'Fine. I know how important it is to Nate and his team to have you on this case. I can assure you that I'll be at the hospital from tomorrow onwards, and there will be no need for our paths to cross again.'

She stopped abruptly and the bleak look in her eyes did little to dissipate the churning sensation low in his gut.

He lost sense of time, unsure how long they remained where they stood across the room from each other, neither of them saying a word. The silence seemed to grow heavier with each passing moment, pressing on them like the heat that wrapped itself around the inhabitants of St Vic just before the storms she had once told him so much about.

Hotter, and tighter, the closer the turbulence drew, and he couldn't help hoping that if he just stayed still, it would pass over them both.

Finally, he felt as though he'd regained some sense of equilibrium and he just about offered a curt dip of his head.

'I'd appreciate that,' he bit out.

And before Talia could answer, he was gone. The door closed softly on its dampeners behind him, doing nothing to diminish the disdain that swirled around him in the wake of his words.

# CHAPTER FIVE

IT COULDN'T REALLY have gone much worse with Liam, Talia decided miserably the next day as she counted the instruments ready for the next surgery.

*Ten sponges.*

The confrontation yesterday had been so unsettling. She should have known he would want to arrive early to give himself a chance to familiarise himself with the clinic and his patient. Typical Liam pragmatism. She was a fool to have taken it personally, letting even a tiny part of herself think that he had come down specifically looking for her.

*Six needle-holders.*

Still, she and Liam now had four days working in the same clinic where they were bound to run into each other. Perhaps starting over would be a good move?

*Two curved forceps.*

Not even that morning's procedure—a Nissen fundoplication to help a patient suffering from gastroesophageal reflux disease—had been enough to stop her from thinking about Liam. She suspected she was going to replay the same doomed conversation—and impossibly hot encounter—over and over in her head for the next month.

Certainly until he left St Victoria.

'Ready, Talia?'

Talia blinked as two of her colleagues entered the sterile area, prepped for surgery. She glanced around the OR and gave a satisfied nod. At least, even with her head filled with thoughts of Liam, she'd completed the pre-surgery routine quickly and systematically.

'Ready,' she confirmed.

But now she had to get her brain straight. Her high level of training meant that while she might be able to get away with a degree of being on autopilot for the prepping, and while this morning she'd been the circulation nurse, this afternoon she was the scrub nurse. Blood clots, bleeding, infection and problems with anaesthesia were all risks associated with the procedure, and as her patient's best advocate in the OR for the next few hours, she could not afford to be distracted by thoughts of her personal life.

Besides, she loved her job, and prided herself on the skills she brought to her role.

Olivia, the surgeon, stepped through the door and Talia concentrated on helping her gown up, and then for the next few hours Talia sank into her role of assisting.

It was lunchtime by the time she was finished

and yet the moment she stepped back outside, it was Liam who was on her mind once again.

The last thing she expected was for him to be waiting for her in the corridor.

'Talia, can I have a moment?'

Her heart thumped hard against her chest wall, but she restrained herself to a mere nod of her head as she wordlessly followed him down the corridor and back to his temporary office. It was useless trying to block out the events of the previous day but she tried all the same.

'Yesterday should never have happened,' he began curtly—his version of an apology. 'Call it jet-lag, or shock at seeing you again, or sheer lack of control, but I shouldn't have let it get that far.'

She twisted her mouth ruefully. They were all plausible excuses for his behaviour, but what about her? She couldn't really claim shock, she'd had been preparing herself for the possibility of seeing him again—however much she'd tried to pretend that transferring to St Vic's would negate that—for weeks. She certainly couldn't blame jet-lag. That only left sheer lack of control. And what did that say about her?

Or either of them, for that matter?

'No,' she agreed. 'I shouldn't have either.'

'I would rather that it didn't happen again.'

As though it was some insignificant thing, and not the fact that she'd broken apart in his hands.

'Of course.' She drew in a steadying breath,

wishing it didn't hurt so much. 'Like I said, we have four more days to get through where our paths may well cross and then, after that, I'll be on the other side of Williamtown.'

'So you mentioned.' He dipped his head but she couldn't make out his tone. It was too even, too neutral. 'However, I wanted to talk to you about that.'

'Oh?'

She couldn't have said why her pulse kicked up the way that it did. And there was no reason at all for her skin to prickle or for that strange sensation, which couldn't possibly be excitement, to ripple down her spine.

'I understand Lucy Wells was originally your patient, which is how you knew the case well enough in the first instance?'

'She was.' Talia lifted her shoulders. 'But once she was accepted for this trial she became part of the clinical trial team's caseload.'

And she knew he would have been poring over all their notes, ensuring he knew the case inside out. He always liked to be as thorough as he possibly could be, whether the surgery was an emergency, or an elective. It was part of what made him so good at what he did.

'But you aren't on that clinical team?' He frowned. 'Why not? You've been an OR nurse in these types of procedures before back at Duke's. With me.'

Talia's mind spun, a thousand replies all cramming her brain at once. But what would be the point in any of them? She'd already said more than she'd ever intended. In the end, she settled for the practical.

'The previous cardiothoracic surgeon had his preferred team from before I even arrived at The Island Clinic, and I wasn't part of it.'

Liam frowned at her again, but this time it felt different.

There was a beat of quiet.

'Did you want to be on the team?'

She blinked, taking a moment to process the question.

'Sure, it's a fascinating surgery and Lucy's a good kid.'

'As far as I'm concerned, you're one of the best scrub nurses I've had in my OR,' he said candidly. 'Isak would be a fool not to want you on the team.'

Gratitude and something else she didn't care to identify shot through Talia. In spite of all they'd just said to one another, he still didn't think twice about telling her that she was a good nurse.

'Thank you.' She pulled her lips together. 'But I also don't know much about the procedure.'

He frowned.

'You've been part of atrial repairs before back at Duke's. With me even.'

'None of the surgeries I was ever on with you

were total atrial arch reconstructions.' She shook her head. 'I've worked on a handful of traditional two-stage elephant trunk procedures, but you're skilled in the single-stage approach.'

'I didn't realise,' he mused, and a heavy weight of regret plummeted through her.

After what had happened in his office less than twenty-four hours ago, it might have been good to have something less…intimate between them. Maybe even get them back to an easier, more neutral footing with each other.

But now he was going to rescind his offer to put her on his team, and she felt a stab of regret. He opened his mouth to speak and she steeled herself for the inevitable.

'Well, you're going to have to learn at some time. I'd still like you on my team.' Liam shrugged, as though it was no big deal. 'So if you want on, I'll talk to Nate in the morning.'

She could almost feel the silence in the room, swirling around her.

'Why? Why are you doing this for me?' He didn't answer, and she was forced to carry on. 'Is this about last night?'

'I don't make decisions about my OR for personal reasons.' He looked distinctly unimpressed, and she knew what he must be thinking. She knew that was true better than anyone else. 'My patients deserve the best team they can get. I've no doubt Isak's team is brilliant but I haven't worked with them all before. I have, however, worked with you and I rate your skills highly. So, as the surgeon running this operation, you are a logical choice.'

Talia couldn't contain her smile, though she cursed her heart for the way it leapt in her chest. He was still prepared to give her a chance, and it struck her as so typically Liam that no matter how badly the two of them were communicating on a personal level, when it came to surgeries, he was the most approachable surgeon she could ever hope to work with.

Professional, and generous with his time and knowledge. Not every surgeon could boast those same qualities. A pang of emotion shot through her, and she could only put it down to some kind of wistful nostalgia.

'And regarding what happened yesterday...?'

She'd never been known for her poker face, but if only she could display even a fraction of the reserve that Liam had.

He was paying her a professional compliment, not a personal one, though that didn't seem to matter to her weak-willed organs. And it was typical Liam to put his patient before every-thing else. It certainly didn't mean he wanted her around for his own purposes, she wasn't going to be foolish enough to let herself think otherwise. No matter how much that traitorous part of her might want to.

'We both said things I think we'd rather take back, but we can't. Therefore I propose we put it behind us and move on.'

By 'it', she presumed he meant the kiss…and more. Was she being perverse, wanting to remind him once again that this was exactly the problem? The way he moved past personal issues but never actually tackled the source?

Maybe, maybe not. She shrugged inwardly. But the last thing she wanted was another row. Shoving her personal feelings down, she offered a tentative nod.

'You're right, we're different people now. Whatever went wrong between us back then, it's long since buried.'

'Agreed,' he answered, too easily for her peace of mind.

She forced herself to smile.

'It doesn't matter anymore.'

'Precisely,' Liam approved, and she hated his matter-of-fact tone, without even a trace of fondness. Especially when she couldn't fight back those unwelcome waves of nostalgia. 'So shall we grab a coffee and you can tell me what you know?'

'Sure.' Talia drew in a steadying breath. This was her moment to prove herself and she wasn't about to blow it. Of all the surgeons to learn from, Liam was certainly one of the best.

It felt odd, walking with him down the hospital

corridors. As if everyone was looking and could read what had already happened between them when logically she knew they couldn't know.

Clearing her throat, she fought to sound purely professional. 'I understand this technique allows you to combine the traditional two-stage surgical and endovascular procedures for complex aortic lesions into a single surgery.'

'Shall we wait until we sit down?' he suggested dryly.

'No.' She shook her head, and took another breath. The sooner she put things onto a professional footing, the better.

Were they walking too close to each other? Should she move out to the side more, or would that look too obvious?

'This trial is to see how recent advances in the right anterior mini-thoracotomy approach mean reduced post-op pain and faster patient recovery, among other benefits, right?'

'Right,' he concurred as they reached the cafeteria. 'Do you want to find a table while I get the coffees?'

She could feel even more eyes on them. Scrutinising them. No doubt she'd be subjected to any number of interrogations from colleagues after this, ranging from curious to downright jealous. Like at Duke's, it was clear that Liam had attracted plenty of attention.

Not that she cared, Talia reminded herself hastily, they were just friends. Whatever had happened yesterday.

'Your coffee, you still take it milk, no sugar?'

'That's fine, *Dr* Miller.' She hastily took the drink, and ignored the odd look he cast her way. 'So, anyway, there are a couple of different kinds of prostheses, too, aren't there?'

He only hesitated a fraction of a moment but it was enough to make her feel foolish. What was she doing, letting other people dictate how she reacted, especially when she thought about Liam's father? The irony of it didn't escape her. She forged on regardless.

'I've been reading the notes from previous operations for this trial and I noticed that with an open prosthesis a one-thirty-millimetre stented graft...'

'Talia, this is ridiculous.'

'...is used with the supra-aortic vessels implanted as....'

'Talia,' he repeated, 'what's going on?'

'I...' heat suffused her cheeks.

'Is this going to be a problem for you? Working with me on this case?'

Panic shot through her. His expression was closed, giving nothing away as usual, yet there was an edge in his tone that she didn't recognise. If she had to guess, she might have thought it was disapproval.

'I'm sorry,' she blurted out hastily. 'I'm just… aware that people are watching us.'

'I'm the stand-in surgeon for the great Isak Nilsson.' Liam shrugged. 'People are going to be interested.'

'Do you think they know?' she muttered into the coffee cup. 'Do you think they can tell?'

Whatever she'd been expecting, it hadn't been Liam's forthright reply.

'That we were intimate yesterday? I don't think they can tell that, no. Though they might guess if you look any more furtive.'

She couldn't answer, though she could feel the heat racing over her skin.

'Talia, we're here legitimately discussing a mutual patient. If you don't want people to gossip then stop looking edgy and don't give them a reason to.'

All at once, her sense of discomfort and guilt morphed into old feelings of frustration and hurt and she swallowed down the urge to scream. The simple truth was that she didn't want to be here with Liam in the clinic cafeteria, discussing a patient.

She would far, far rather have been back in the privacy of his office or, better still, in the suite he'd been allocated in the clinic's luxury hotel, which was well equipped to deal with entire Hollywood entourages, let alone a single surgeon.

And she would far rather have been engaged

in more diverting activities than discussing a patient—as much as she wanted the best for Lucy Wells.

But such a fantasy was pointless. Liam had already been more than explicit that yesterday's intimacy had been a mistake not to be repeated. He didn't want her.

But she, to her shame, still wanted him.

'Did you know Nate has provided me with a chauffeur-driven car to give me a tour around the island?' Liam asked her, without warning. 'Apparently, your chief thinks it's important for me to get to know more about the island.'

And, in spite of everything, Talia laughed. The idea of Liam exploring an island when he could be working on a new, challenging operation was almost laughable. But how typical of Nate to encourage it, all the same.

'He's proud of the island.' She grinned suddenly. 'We all are. And you have a reputation for burying yourself in your work, so I imagine he's trying to ensure you take some time out, too. Then again, he could be hoping you might take a swing by St Vic's Hospital. They're always in need of medical staff to offer their time for free.'

'And do you?' asked Nate. 'Offer your time free.'

'Whenever I can,' she confirmed with another grin.

She liked it that it seemed to catch him off

guard for a moment. But she wasn't ready when he turned around and did the same.

'Fancy showing me around?' he asked abruptly.

Her entire body felt as though she'd slammed into a wall. She didn't want to consider why that might be.

'Me?' she asked tentatively. 'Why?'

'Maybe we can find some common ground, make it easier to work together.'

He even offered her a bright, airy smile, his voice even and unaffected, but she hadn't missed that pause for a fraction of a second first.

'You always promised me a guided tour,' he pushed when she didn't answer. Though she wanted to. So very badly.

'Over three years ago,' she managed instead.

'And now here we are. So, how about we meet outside The Island Clinic entrance, any morning this week at eight? I seem to remember we were both always early risers.'

She flicked her tongue over her lips and pretended she couldn't understand Liam well enough to know that he'd felt a punch of victory. His words had been designed to hit their mark. To remind her of the number of mornings they'd woken before their alarm and spent the last possible moment in bed, making love.

'Liam—'

'I seem to remember a St Victoria native once

recommending that a good place to start would be the Beics.'

'I didn't think you ever listened to me,' she said shortly.

'I listened,' he said with another smile.

'Well,' she scraped around for another excuse. Anything. 'I didn't think you'd have any free time. You're usually buried in work.'

'Aren't you the one who always told me the pace of life was different, here on St Victoria?' he challenged her. 'And according to your chief, his focus is on quality over quantity.'

Yes, she could well imagined Nate having given Liam plenty of challenging cases, but also a fair amount of downtime.

'So let me know which morning suits you,' Liam continued. 'And I'll see you then.'

Talia met his steady gaze right then, and didn't know if what she saw in them was a promise or something far, far, greater. But, then, it didn't matter. She stared at him for another long moment before finally pushing herself to her feet and picking up her still half-full coffee cup.

'I'll think about it,' she bit out, wishing her heart wasn't leaping around in such delight.

'I'll take that as better than a flat-out *no.*'

'It isn't a *yes*, either,' she pointed out. Though she suspected they both new how tempted she was.

On all counts.

# CHAPTER SIX

'THE SURGEON SAID something about whirlpool signs? I just don't understand exactly what he wants to do to Obi.'

Obi's mother's voice pitched upwards in panic and Talia fought to smother the irritation that swelled inside her at thought of the departing paediatric surgeon.

The guy was evidently in far too much of a hurry to get back on the helicopter that would take him out of the community hospital and back to the unmistakable luxury of The Island Clinic. Clearly, he was far too keen to return to fawning over all his A-list clientele, to take the time to simplify a complex procedure for a concerned mother.

He was a brilliant surgeon but not a very pleasant man who had never been a fan of The Island Clinic-St Vic's outreach programme, which would bring eight-year-old Obi to The Island Clinic for her surgery.

It was why he wasn't going to last long with Nate as Chief of Staff. Whereas Liam…

An image of Liam popped, uninvited, into Talia's brain and she found it was impossible not to compare one man with the other. If this had been a cardiothoracic case, and young Obi had been one of his patients, Liam would never have left a panicked mother with a bunch of unanswered questions.

She heard that only the previous night, Liam had spent a good couple of hours with Lucy Wells, and her mother, Violet. Explaining things in detail and answering all their questions. He was so skilled at pitching things just right. Simplifying things just enough for a lay person, without becoming condescending.

Talia could never imagine the mother of one if his patients being so confused.

But Obi wasn't Liam's case, and letting her mind wander to him served no purpose other than to distract herself. Hastily she turned her attention back to Obi's mother.

'That's why I'm here,' Talia soothed quickly, reaching out to take the young woman's hands in her own. 'I'm your liaison between here and The Island Clinic, and I'm here to explain anything I can.'

Obi was a local girl who had been diagnosed at birth with congenital intestinal malrotation, but whose condition hadn't previously been serious enough to warrant surgical intervention before now.

The girl had recently begun presenting with abdominal pain of a chronic and diffuse nature, and the team at St Vic's had conducted a series of medical images to determine the position of the duodenum and the proximal small bowel, as well as looking for the 'whirlpool' sign typical of volvulus.

'Sonography has revealed that a part of Obi's gut has now twisted around on itself completely—that's the whirlpool sign the surgeon mentioned—which has changed her medical status from asymptomatic to acute, and which now necessitates surgery. She will be flown to The Island Clinic tonight—we have family accommodation for you to stay, so don't worry—and a nasogastric tube will be inserted through Obi's nose into her stomach and placed on low intermittent suction; we will ensure any fluid or electrolyte deficits are corrected and she will be placed on broad-spectrum antibiotics before surgery.'

'Because she has appendicitis, too?' the mother asked anxiously.

'No.' Talia shook her head gently. 'Actually, it's the contrary. During the procedure, the intestine will be straightened out to reduce that so-called whirlpool effect, and the small intestine will be folded into the right side of the abdomen while the large bowel—or colon—will go on the left-hand side. Now, usually the appendix would be found on the right side of the abdomen, but where there is intestinal malrotation it has often moved to the left.'

'So it would be in the way.'

'Although it is rare, there is always a possibility that the artery to the appendix could be damaged in the course of the surgery,' Talia conceded. 'But the other reason is because, should Obi ever develop appendicitis in the future, the atypical location of it could complicate diagnosis and treatment.'

For a further half-hour Talia continued to answer questions, feeling a sense of deep satisfaction as she managed to calm the understandably frightened mother and prepare her for the short flight to The Island Clinic with her young daughter.

Finally, the two of them emerged from the quiet consultation room, and Talia headed back to the nurses' station to go through other patient notes before she, too, left St Vic's Hospital.

'Talia, girl, haven't seen you for too long. How've you been doin' up at that posh Island Clinic of yours?'

Talia snapped her head up from her notes as she was greeted by one of St Vic's longest-serving staff. She was an older woman who was both fun and friendly to work with, and an experienced nurse.

'Nyla.' She let the woman embrace her in a

crushing hug. 'It's been good up there, though I've been here in the community clinic from time to time, but we've kept crossing shifts. Don't tell me we'll finally be working together?'

'No,' Nyla said mournfully. 'I've been on night shift. I'm heading off in half an hour.'

'Oh, no,' commiserated Talia, genuinely sorry. It would have been good to have a shift with Nyla. Perhaps it would have helped to take her mind off anything *Liam*-related. 'Who's going to give me all the up-to-date gossip?'

'Well, we've got half an hour to make the most of it.' The older woman's eyes gleamed and Talia realised, too late, that the gossip was going to be about her. 'So I understand the new clinic surgeon is your old beau.'

'Don't know what you mean.' Talia shook her head, wishing that she was a better liar.

Or at least that Nyla wasn't so damned shrewd.

'Oh, girl, don't even try to feed me that line.' Nyla shot her an empathetic look. 'I can read you too well, child. But if it makes you feel any better, no one else up there has any idea, they're all too busy trying to snag him for theyselves.'

'Then how did you know?' She was genuinely curious.

Nyla tapped her nose and laughed. *'Boonoonoonoos!'*

'He's not my special friend, Nyla.' Talia wrinkled her nose.

'Sure he is. You know me, I've always had a sense for this stuff. The moment I saw your pinched little face from across that corridor, it all fell into place. The new doc from North Carolina, the fact that you suddenly got you'self transferred here for a rotation, the way you look as though you're about to jump out of you' own skin any minute.'

'I do not.' Talia frowned defensively, then shook her head at her own blunder. 'Okay, maybe a little.'

'So he is the one who hurt you.' Nyla raised her eyebrows knowingly.

A week ago, Talia wouldn't have thought twice about confirming it. Now, though, his words rang in her head.

'Yeah.' She nodded slowly, then pulled a face. 'Though if you'd heard him speak the other day, you'd have thought I was the one at fault.'

As usual, the words were out before she could stop them but instead of looking surprised Nyla gave a half-shout of delight.

'We knew it.'

'Sorry?'

'Your mama and I, we always knew it.' Nyla reached a plump arm out and squeezed Talia's shoulders. 'We al'ays said he be a fool to hurt you; maybe he is hurting a little himself, no?'

'You and Mama said that?'

'Sho' we did.' Nyla nodded triumphantly. 'It

took him all his time to come after you, but we al'ays thought he would.'

Whatever foolish glimmer had made her heart thump like a dog's tail feebly wagging for a scrap was snuffed out in an instant.

'No.' She shook her head, trying to sound resolute rather than miserable. Not that she wouldn't have trusted Nyla to see a little of the torment she was putting herself through, but if she let it in, even just a little, what if she couldn't shut it off again.

'He didn't come here for me.' Talia forced a smile. 'He came here for a case. Nate picked him.'

'Yet he knew this is where you were?'

'Not exactly.' Talia frowned, remembering Liam's words. 'He didn't know where I'd gone.'

Nyla let out an incredulous bark of laughter.

'You believe that, girl? 'Course he knew. This is your home, where else would you be? And after all, he's here now, isn't he?'

'He isn't here for me,' Talia reiterated, though perhaps more for herself than for Nyla.

What was the point in false hope? She would only get hurt again.

'I see.' The older woman nodded sagely. 'He said that, did he?'

'Yes. We had an argument and he was painfully clear.'

'Aye.'

There wasn't explicit encouragement in Nyla's tone, yet Talia heard it all the same. And she couldn't help herself from admitting more.

'Then we apologised…' She bit her lip. 'He offered me a place on the operating team.'

Nyla didn't say anything. She didn't have to. Eyeing her triumphant expression, Talia felt that tiny flame of hope flicker back into life.

'He asked me if I'd show him around the island. I said that I'd think about it because it can't be a wise idea, can it?'

Another sage glance from Nyla had a grin spreading, uncontained, over Talia's face. She felt the corners of her lips being pulled up, an almost lightness invading her body, swiftly followed by a veritable kaleidoscope of butterflies.

'You think I should go, don't you?' she asked Nyla, who threw up her hands in true dramatic fashion.

'Don't ask me, child, I'm just here to listen. If *you* think you should go, that's what matters.'

It was hardly the instruction Talia had been looking for, but that didn't seem to matter. She was shuffling her notes and moving as though spurred into some—any—kind of action.

'I'll go and see if my patient and her family have arrived,' Talia declared.

'And shall I get the number of the hotel room where the new doc is staying?' demanded Nyla dryly. 'You can pop up there after your shift.'

'No need,' Talia sang out, already making her way along the corridor to the waiting area. 'I have their number on my phone anyway. I can just call and leave him a message. It doesn't have to be a bigger deal that that.'

Because it *wasn't* a bigger deal that that, Talia decided firmly. It was two old friends setting aside personal differences and being professional. He was handing her an olive branch by offering her a place on his operating team, there was no reason why she shouldn't do the same by showing him around the island.

*Her* island.

It was no more, no less than that.


'So these are the Beics,' Talia told him, two days later, as she pointed across the breath-taking, aquamarine waters of the bay. 'Three volcanic peaks, or plugs, are linked by the Bec Ridge. The smallest one is around two thousand, two hundred feet high, while the tallest is just shy of three thousand feet.'

'And they're called the Beics because they look like bird beaks?' Liam guessed, trying to pretend his body wasn't reacting to her all-too-familiar shampoo scent of coconut and hibiscus.

The way he'd been fighting against doing that all morning.

'Exactly.' She laughed that soft laugh of hers.

'You have Petit Bec and Grand Bec, which I guess speak for themselves, and then the jagged middle-sized one is known as Bec Dentelé.'

That laugh did things to him that he felt it had no business doing. He tried to push it out of his head, but it was proving impossible. His senses were already on overload and he couldn't seem to shut them down.

St Victoria was stunning, and loud, and vibrant. It oozed life and fun out of every bright, laughter-filled street, every evocative steel band, and every incredible view. And every bit of it reminded him of how Talia had seemed to blow into Duke's, four years ago, filling his world with sound and splashing vibrant colour all over the dull walls of his previously black and white life. How he'd felt like he was being brought to life— when he hadn't even realised he'd needed to be.

It had felt...*right.*

For possibly the first time in his life, he'd felt... if not love then certainly care. Tenderness. And although it had felt strange at first, he'd found himself quickly growing accustomed to it, liking it, even beginning to return it.

But then, without warning, she'd disappeared as abruptly as she'd arrived, and everything had faded to monochrome again in an instant. Only this time Liam had known what he was missing, which had only made it seem all the bleaker. All the emptier.

He'd be damned if he was going to let that happen again. He'd come here to take this new case, not to seek out old demons, but if he was going to have to face them here, he had no intention of letting them get the better of him a second time.

'I seem to recall you once telling me that you can climb the Bec Range?'

'Yeah, you can hike them easily enough, especially Petit Bec and Grand Bec, and the ridge isn't too bad to cross.'

'And lots of tourists visit for the hot springs.'

Too late, he tried to swallow back the statement. It felt too personal, too intimate somehow. A hark back to the conversations they'd once shared as a couple, when she used to talk about her home, and when they both imagined him one day coming to see it with her.

As though they'd really believed in that future.

'Right.' She swallowed hard, as if she was trying to shake the same memories. 'But you have to be careful of the fumaroles.'

His mind latched onto the safer topic as he searched for something less personal to say.

'So you get a few burns at the hospital, especially in tourist season?'

Her mouth crinkled up and he pretended that he didn't notice.

'You always have your surgeon's head on, don't you? Yes, we do get cases at the hospital. But there are some great guided tours available, you don't have to risk life and limb to visit them.'

'I'll bear that in mind,' he offered sardonically, wishing he didn't overthink every statement she made.

Was that why she'd left him? Because he was always focussed on his patients and his career? And if that was true, why did he even care what she thought?

Why did he want to spin her around and ask her why she'd really put his name forward to her chief of staff? Had it really been about her patient? Or had there been a part of her that had wanted to see him again?

Because, however much it galled him to admit it, there was certainly a part of him that wondered. And he hated it that she haunted him in this way.

'Of course, there are plenty of other places to visit if you're nervous.'

Her wry voice cut through the air and he blinked, the cogs in his mind trying to recall the last part of their conversation.

'Nervous?' he rasped out.

'If you don't trust me not to lead us into any dangerous fumaroles?'

'Ah, I see.' He could think of being places with

Talia that were a damned sight more dangerous than mere fumaroles.

And even though he knew she was teasing him—even though he knew it wasn't a wise idea to respond—he couldn't help himself.

'I'm game if you are. Besides, you also promised to take me scuba diving on the reefs, and ziplining from the rainforest canopy.'

Her gaze turned to him, seeming to almost burn into him, but he could work out what she was thinking. Her dark eyes, the colour of the richest cacao, had often been an enigma to him.

For several long moments they simply watched each other. Liam wasn't even sure if he stopped breathing. And then, at last, she broke the silence, her voice perhaps a little too unnaturally breezy.

'What did you think of Lucy Wells? I heard you finally had chance to meet her in person.'

He cast her a thoughtful glance.

'She's clearly a bright kid. And mature for fifteen. But then, given her medical condition, that's understandable.'

'True,' Talia nodded. 'And Violet?'

He knew what she was doing, trying to get the conversation onto a professional footing. But it wasn't territory in which he was comfortable. He wasn't the only surgeon who liked to meet his patients and get some understanding of who they were yet didn't generally like to consider their personal circumstances too deeply.

If surgeries didn't quite go to plan, it could sometimes make it hard to make the difficult decisions.

'Violet is clearly a mother who fiercely loves her daughter, but I was surprised at how pragmatic she is, too.'

Talia nodded.

'Not the overbearing Hollywood type you were expecting? Throwing her money or power around?'

'I try not to pre-judge,' he grimaced. 'But I suppose that's true enough.'

He was grateful when Talia didn't press the matter. Another gentle silence swirled around them, until she spoke again.

'So, the island really is a place of two halves. Approximately eight hundred square kilometres from the wild yet quiet mini-jungle at one end, and the noisy, bustling city of the historic centre nearer the other.'

'Impressive,' he acknowledged. 'Anything else?'

They both knew he wasn't referring to the sightseeing tour, though he didn't know why he was trying to make things more personal. Shouldn't he be relieved that Talia had been working so hard to keep things on a neutral footing?

'No more facts about the flora?' He heard his quiet challenge. 'The fauna?'

*What was wrong with him?*

Talia's eyes locked with his, a flicker of uncertainty under all that smoky heat. She licked her lips even as her eyebrow arched up.

'I could tell you that around three hundred plant species have been identified on the Beics, ten of them rare, as well as some thirty-odd bird species.'

He didn't miss the slight hitch in her voice, however, and he suppressed a smile. At least he wasn't the only one finding the entire day awkward.

Like a date that they'd never actually had.

*Don't even go there,* he warned himself hastily.

'So you're happy back here?' he asked abruptly.

Hardly an improvement. He wasn't surprised when Talia snapped her head around to him.

'Sorry?'

He didn't repeat the question, there seemed little point.

'I like it back here,' she hazarded after a moment. 'It…isn't as bad as I once thought.'

He assumed she was referring to all the times she'd told him that she hadn't been able to stand living on St Victoria. That moving to the States, to somewhere like North Carolina, had been like a dream to her.

'You once said that you would never come back here. That it was too small, too insular.'

'I was wrong,' she bit back. 'About a lot of things.'

He frowned. It sounded as though she was having a go at him, but he couldn't imagine for what.

'You're referring to me? You were wrong about me?'

She shrugged, but didn't answer.

'I thought I was about the only thing that remained consistent throughout,' he pressed, not liking the inference but unable to put his finger on quite why it rankled the way it did.

'Is that what you think?' she demanded suddenly.

'I told you who I was, what I believed, from the outset. I never wavered on that.'

She glared at him for another long moment.

'No.' She blew out a breath at last. Long and heartfelt. 'I don't suppose you did.'

But it sounded less appreciative than Liam might have expected. And then she threw herself back in the seat and turned her head to stare out of the window, the conversation clearly over.

So much for trying to establish some kind of working connection.

*Because, of course, this was what today had been about,* that sly voice insinuated in his head.

He found he didn't care for it much. He cared even less for the fact that it was right. Accepting the medical case had been as much about coming to Talia's home island as it had been about the challenging surgery. And that, in itself, was an issue.

Yet, like every other reservation he'd had in the past couple of weeks, Liam thrust it aside and turned back to the creature he couldn't seem to shake from his head, no matter how he tried.

'Okay, where now?'

'Now?' She didn't exactly squeak it, but her voice sounded a fraction higher than normal.

She cleared her throat again and checked her watch. Liam suspected it was more for something to do than because she actually needed to. Still, a faintly relieved expression skittered over her lovely features as she realised the time, tapping on the panel to the driver and issuing some polite instruction before sitting back in her seat next to him.

'Now we go and get lunch.'

# CHAPTER SEVEN

BEING WITH LIAM was even harder than she'd anticipated, Talia admitted to herself an hour later as they threaded their way through the colourful, loud Williamtown streets. And she hadn't expected it to be easy to start with.

She'd tried to be a good guide, showing him the St Victoria that she would have been proud to show to any other visiting surgeon. But, then, Liam wasn't any other surgeon, was he? He was Liam Miller, the man who had always been able to twist her inside out.

It seemed that nothing had changed.

It didn't help that the tour itself felt altogether too much like a date. At least, it did to her. So much for having told herself that it was just two old friends offering an olive branch to each other, no more and no less. Who had she been kidding, anyway? They'd laughed their way around the island—*her* island—and it had felt good.

And odd.

And conflicting.

Seeing St Victoria through his eyes had been something of a revelation. Almost a chance to see the island afresh. And, in line with everything she'd been feeling more and more this past year, she began to wonder why she'd ever been so desperate to leave in the first place. Or why, when she'd felt those pangs of homesickness in North Carolina, she'd stuffed them down and instructed herself that they hadn't existed.

She pretended that she didn't know that the answer to the latter was walking right beside her. So close she could actually feel the heat bouncing off his body into hers. Seeping right through to her very bones and making her wonder if—as mad as it sounded—should he suddenly turn around over lunch and ask her to return to Duke's with him she wouldn't agree.

Could she really sacrifice the island that held her soul for the man who held her heart? Because, whatever she'd pretended to herself, the truth was that he did still hold it. She could claim she was over him as much as she liked, but it didn't make it true.

*Some tour guide you are,* she berated herself, trying to drag her focus back to the task in hand.

They were going for lunch.

Nothing more intimate that that.

And yet it didn't feel that easy. Everywhere they turned, people were laughing, smiling, welcoming them. She hoped Liam didn't have enough patois to understand what was being aimed their way, people clearly seeing them as some kind of couple.

Even now, a handful of street vendors was trying to tempt them with local cuisine cooked right in front of them as they addressed them as the *happy newlyweds*. Talia squeezed her eyes shut. Tightly.

It terrified her how utterly seduced she was by that simple notion. Even now—all these years on.

She shook her head in frustration.

'Talia?' His hand curved around her elbow, strong and steadying. 'Everything okay?'

The last thing she needed…and the very thing she wanted. Sensations charged around her body like volts of electricity.

She sucked in a deep breath and somehow—she would never know how—spun quickly so that it wrenched at the contact without looking as though that was what she'd intended at all.

'I'm fine.' She smiled brightly and convinced herself that she looked serene and happy—not like some demented grinning gecko.

Liam cast her a sceptical glance.

'What's happened? A moment ago we were getting on well, now suddenly you seem…edgy.'

'Nonsense.' Even she didn't find her sing-song voice believable.

'Do you want to try that again, only this time with more feeling?'

She didn't want to laugh, she didn't even want to smile. It was too painful to realise how easily he could still read her.

'Go on,' he encouraged, clearly sensing her weakening. 'I'll feed you the line again. Talia, everything okay?'

'Idiot.' She batted his arm lightly with her hand, the corners of her mouth twitching upwards all the same.

'Better,' he approved, and warmth flowed through her.

She told herself that she hated how something so simple from him could affect her. Perversely, it made her want to say something to get under his skin, too. Just to prove to herself that she wasn't the only one on edge today, despite how well it had seemed to have been going.

'If you must know...' she craned her neck up to look at him '...they were calling us *newlyweds.*'

To his credit, Liam didn't back away the way she'd expected him to. That didn't mean to say she couldn't feel that momentary tension from his body.

'I see.'

'They think we look loved up.'

Her heart felt as though it was climbing up her chest and into her throat, but Talia stuffed it back down. Memories of the other day still flooded her body every night, it was hardly surprising that they'd flood her mind right now, too.

'I suppose we might look like a couple,' he conceded at last, to her surprise.

She twisted her neck all the more.

'It doesn't bother you more?'

'Should it?'

'The last time I even voiced anything to do with marriage, you told me that it was an out-dated institution that wasn't for you.'

He actually looked shocked and, for a moment, she thought she must have imagined that entire nightmare conversation of three years ago. Then, at last, his expression cleared.

'And that made you think I wouldn't want to hear someone calling us *newlyweds*?'

She lifted her shoulders, no longer quite as certain.

'It crossed my mind. We seem to have been getting on so well that I didn't want anything to… spoil it. Besides, I know how you pride yourself on your reputation for professionalism.'

'You're giving me a guided tour—we're hardly walking down the street, giving people a public show,' he answered, but his voice was tighter than before and Talia knew the conversation was getting to him.

She wanted to stop it, but it was like opening the lid on an ant farm—impossible to get everything back in.

'No, but still…' She splayed her hands out when words failed her.

There was so much more she wanted to ask— to know—but this was hardly the time or place.

Perhaps nowhere ever would be now. It was too far in the past.

But, still, as she watched him, a hundred thoughts swirling around her head, she got the feeling he was trying to pull himself back to the present.

It was shameful how fervently she wished she knew what he'd been thinking.

'I think—'

'Perhaps it would be better to abandon this conversation.' He cut her off with forced joviality. 'Get back to where we were a few minutes ago.'

It was more of an instruction than a question and Talia wondered what he would say if she pressed the point.

But the truth was that she didn't want to. Today had been so nice, so comfortable, with Liam that she didn't want to ruin it now. She wanted to hold onto it, for as long as they could.

'Right.' It was all she could do to match his level of conviviality. To motivate her body back into action and keep them moving through the market. 'Good idea.'

As if her heart wasn't breaking inside all over again.

It shouldn't surprise her that he was pushing her away again, she told herself. And it really shouldn't dismay her at all.

Heat shimmered in the already searing air as mouth-watering scents floated tantalisingly towards Liam. One vendor offered some sort of stunning salt-fish dish, another had a glorious soup that appeared to be made from a plant Talia teased him about not even properly recognising.

Yet he felt as though he was moving through a fug.

He'd felt like this all day, all week. Ever since that kiss in his office, if he was being honest. And this latest conversation hadn't helped. Reminding him that, in spite of every bad thing he knew about marriage, and family, and despite every promise he'd made to himself never to go down such a destructive route, three years ago he'd actually entertained the notion of asking Talia to spend the rest of her life with him.

When she'd left, he'd convinced himself it was if not a good thing then at least for the best. But now that he was here in St Victoria, with Talia, it was becoming harder and harder to remember that.

And though Liam didn't care to examine why, he could feel this thing that had begun to hum inside him and he couldn't—didn't *want to*—switch it off. A cadence, a rhythm he hadn't heard in such a long time, like the way the air seemed to pulse with the beat of the fantastic steel drums being played in the park across the way. The marketplace bustling with life and colour, as though the hurricane of several years ago was nothing more than a distant memory, though he remembered it from the news and from the little Talia had told him.

He didn't like to press her on it. She was clearly trying to lighten the mood from a moment ago, and doing a better job of it than he was.

'The fried plantains are good. As is the bread-fruit when it's mashed with coconut milk and baked in banana leaves like that.' Talia's voice broke through his thoughts, causing a fresh kick inside his chest before he reined it back under control.

It seemed the day together had made him forget to keep his guard up. Perhaps, for both their sakes, he ought to remedy that but he couldn't seem to bring himself to do it.

'I recall you telling me once before.' He smiled.

She blinked at him in surprise.

'I did?'

'You did,' he confirmed. 'Back at Hal's Diner, round the corner from Duke's—you remember? We were having breakfast one morning and you looked at your pancakes and pondered what you wouldn't give to have a forkful of coconut milk breadfruit for once.'

'Oh.'

'You suggested that, should we ever visit your family, you'd introduce me to some typical St Victoria culinary delights.'

The air shimmered between them, only this

time it had nothing to do with the food being prepared.

He recognised only too well the way that she pulled her mouth a fraction to one side. He just didn't know what it meant.

Had his stirring up of old memories somehow spoiled what had otherwise been a pleasant—more than pleasant—day? Ruining things between them?

*Just like you did last time.*

The smug voice came out of nowhere, its almost triumphant tone echoing around his head. A voice which, Liam considered abruptly, sounded remarkably like his father's voice.

He stared around the square, almost as though he expected the old man to materialise at any time. But this wasn't Duke's, or even North Carolina, where Donald Miller seemed to haunt his every move, even though he'd learned long ago that he had to cut all ties to such a toxic old man.

No, this wasn't back there—a place he didn't even think of as *home.* This was St Victoria, a Caribbean island so far from home that it felt like a whole other life. And maybe here, Liam realised with a jolt, he could be someone different. Someone other than the man whose every decision in life had to make up for the way his mother had lost hers.

Just for a while.

He turned to Talia, but whatever he might

have been about to say next froze on his lips as he caught sight of a kid racing straight towards Talia. The language was partly patois, but Liam caught enough to know that a man had been hit by a car in a nearby street and a neighbour, having seen Talia at the market earlier, had sent the boy to find her.

Neither of them waited to hear any more. Almost in unison, they both instructed the boy to lead the way, hurrying behind the kid without a word needing to be spoken. Slipping back into that old working harmony they'd once shared, as if it was an old friend.

By the time they arrived, an ambulance—one of the four new highly equipped donations from The Island Clinic—was already on scene, and it took Liam and Talia little time to ascertain that the man had indeed been involved in a car-versus-pedestrian collision, with the man having been anaesthetised before for transport. However, before he had been able to be loaded onto the ambulance, he'd gone into cardiac arrest and the team had pushed fluids into him via a drip, as well as beginning CPR, with no response.

Watching another round of CPR being carried out, Liam was all too aware that time was running out for the patient, and although it was a great effort by the team already on scene, if they were unable to get his heart restarted there would be little point in loading him into the ambulance for St Vic's.

'What are you going to do?' Talia placed her hand on his arm as he stepped forward through the crowd.

He dropped back, lowering his head so no one could overhear. No use in panicking anyone else around.

'If they can't resuscitate him this time then there's only one other option I can think of...'

'You're going to open him up here? On the street?' Talia nodded. 'Massage his heart to try to get it to beat again?'

'It's a bit of a Hail Mary, and the chances of success aren't good,' he admitted, 'but we have to at least try to manage any internal injuries and get his heart restarted.'

Biting her lip, she offered another short nod then stepped after him, pulling aside one of the senior paramedics to introduce Liam as The Island Clinic's cardiothoracic surgeon. He would have had to have done it without her, if she hadn't been around, but there was no doubt that Talia's established relationship with the existing team helped them to accept his solution quicker. And, for this patient, every second counted.

As hastily as he could, Liam sterilised himself and the patient while Talia worked with the paramedic to pull together as much kit as possible, and then he opened up the man's chest and went to work.

Later, much later, he knew he would reflect on how easily and naturally he and Talia had worked together, managing to stem the significant internal bleeding and massaging the man's heart back into rhythm within a matter of mere minutes.

But for the moment all Liam could concentrate on was the patient in front of him, the familiarity of the procedure, despite the circumstances, seeming familiar and oddly soothing.

This part of the heart—the actual physical manifestation of the muscular organ in the human body—was what he could deal with. It was what he understood best.

A world apart from the other, less tangible role of the heart—the emotions and connotations it raised. And those thoughts that had churned through his head earlier—the idea of trying to be someone different from the man he was back in North Carolina—were stronger now.

Life was so short, and so very precious, something he should know more than most. He'd thought he was living his best life being a successful surgeon. Emotions were a weakness, and meant for other people. The effect Talia's leaving had had on him, three years ago, had proved that.

Only now…he wasn't sure it had proved anything of the sort. Now, suddenly, he knew he wanted something else. Something...*more*.

He just didn't know what he was supposed to do with that knowledge.

# CHAPTER EIGHT

'SMALL YOURSELF UP, Talia.' Nyla squeezed past her at the desk and reached for a bag that had been stuffed underneath. 'Now we finally have a full shift together, I'll show you what my eldest granddaughter brought home the other day, thinking that she was going to wear it.'

Squeezing in to let her colleague pass, Talia welcomed the distraction. Once again, she felt the need to get out of her own head. To get some distance from the questions that were chasing around her brain. Like her island tour with Liam a few days previously.

Was she imagining things to think that he had been more open and more honest with her during those few hours than he'd been during their entire relationship?

It had felt as though they were finally getting closer…right up until the accident had wrenched them away. After that, there had been no time to stop, with Liam even accompanying the man to the hospital to operate on him. Volunteering his time, just as Nate Edwards had always hoped his staff would do.

Talia clenched her jaw tightly, unsure how she

felt about the notion. The more time she spent in his company, the harder it was becoming to keep that lid on all the emotions she'd stuffed down for the past three years.

Liam was every inch as raw and magnetic as he'd been back then. Only now there was that added factor. Something that hadn't been there last time. It made her think that maybe, just maybe, he finally wanted to lower those barriers that had always come between them.

Or perhaps she was just being as foolish as ever and seeing what she wanted to see.

She needed some space to think. A chance to get her head straight.

So for the next few minutes Talia welcomed the distraction of Nyla entertaining her with a pile of clothes, recognisable as coming from the local markets. A veritable wardrobe of garments so tiny that the entire collection could have been kept in little more than a shoebox. Everything that a sixteen-year-old girl might need to look on trend but which a grandmother and parent would consider indecent.

'I mean, look at this skirt.' Nyla held up a flimsy bit of fabric that wasn't much bigger than the head caps they wore in Theatre. 'And what about the bikini?'

'It looks like a handkerchief tied with dental floss.' Talia laughed, wondering how Nyla's granddaughter had even hoped to get away with it.

'It will send all the boys mad.' Nyla threw her hands up.

'It's sort of pretty, though.'

'On a woman like you, perhaps,' scoffed Nyla. 'But not on a kid.'

'I assume you're taking them back to the market stall?' Talia smiled as Nyla put the box away and sat down in front of the computer.

'I am. Maybe between all the items, we can buy her something that she likes but won't be giving me, or her parents, apoplexy.'

'Good luck with that.' She didn't like their chances. 'So, any changes since yesterday?' Talia asked.

'A couple of discharges, several more admitted.' Nyla replied.

'Oh, and Augustin had a pericardiocentesis.' One of the other nurses, Mia, appeared behind her as Talia snapped up from her own notes.

'Augustin? The eleven-year-old who was admitted for pneumonia last week?'

'Yep.' The nurse nodded. 'He deteriorated rapidly last night. Thanks be that Doc Bashy was here to save him.'

'That's enough, Mia,' Nyla cut in quickly.

Perhaps a little too quickly. Talia's stomach began to tense, the way it always did when it was ready to flip-flop.

'Doc Bashy?' she repeated carefully.

Bashy was local slang for hot, or good looking, and while there was no reason for her to suspect Mia meant Liam, her gut was making its feelings loud and clear.

'You haven't met him yet?' Mia let out a long, low whistle. 'Girl, you haven't lived! He's the new surgeon taken over from Isak at The Island Clinic. Apparently, they call him the Heart Whisperer, but we decided he was Doc Bashy... because, he is F-I-N-E *fine*.'

'Okay, that really is enough, Mia,' Nyla repeated. 'Can you go and check on Mrs Frances in bed five, please.'

'Now?' Mia looked surprised, but Nyla was firm.

'Yes, please.'

Talia held herself straight, unmoving, as the younger nurse hurried away, but her mind was already racing. Liam was still here at St Vic's Hospital? Surely he ought to have returned to The Island Clinic by now? Slowly she turned to Nyla.

'I knew he performed a one-off surgery here the other night,' she hazarded. 'Now he's volunteering for full shifts?'

'First one last night,' confirmed Nyla. 'Think he prefers being here to being up there. And now practically every single nurse in this hospital is clamouring to be on his next shift. But none of them know he's your Dr Miller.'

'He isn't my Dr *Anyone*,' Talia managed, her tongue feeling altogether too thick for her mouth. 'Is he still here?'

'Just going off shift,' Nyla replied, though Talia had to strain to hear her. Incredible how hard it was to hear anything over the thundering of her own heart. 'Wait, Talia, is this really what you want to do? Confront him here?'

Talia didn't answer. She was already racing to the changing area doors just as Liam stepped out.

'What happened with Augustin?' she demanded instantly.

Liam paused, and eyed her curiously.

'Good morning to you, too. Is he your patient?'

'Well…' She hesitated, momentarily thrown. 'I was the one who admitted him a few days ago and diagnosed pneumonia.'

'You're a scrub nurse. You're the one who admitted him?'

'The community clinic is a hands-on, all-in affair. Besides, it's good to keep other skills going.'

'I see.'

Without warning, she bristled defensively.

'The symptoms he presented with were consistent with pneumonia.'

'Did I criticise in any way?' Liam asked evenly. It did little to assuage Talia's tenseness.

'No, but—'

'There is no *but*,' he cut in smoothly. 'It was a logical assessment, and the past few days offered no further clues from what I can tell, although there was no improvement. However, overnight his condition deteriorated acutely and he developed more intense chest pains, shortness of breath and diaphoresis. It was fortuitous that I was on the floor, and that the nurse on shift thought to get me.'

A hundred questions jostled on the tip of her tongue, ranging from her patient to why Liam had even been volunteering after claiming he wouldn't.

In the end, it was her concern for Augustin that won out.

'And?'

'The patient was afebrile, with a respiratory rate of thirty-six, he had a heart rate of one-twenty, and blood pressure of one-eighteen over seventy. He hadn't undergone an EKG—'

'Because it presented as pneumonia.'

'Again, I wasn't criticising,' Liam replied simply. 'But since I was there, I performed a bedside ultrasound, in the first instance as a lung ultrasound and, as I suspected, the lungs were obscured by a large anechoic structure.'

Talia sucked in a deep breath. An anechoic structure was often an indication of cysts, fluid or gallbladder ascites. Should she have seen that herself, earlier?

'You carried out a cardiac ultrasound,' she pressed Liam urgently.

'I did.' He nodded. 'It revealed a large circumferential pericardial effusion, right diastolic ventricular collapse and the inferior vena cava was dilated without respiratory variation.'

'So you carried out a pericardiocentesis? What did you yield?'

'About one thousand and fifty millilitres of serosanguinous fluid that have been sent off for further diagnostic evaluation.'

Meaning cultures and cytology, Talia thought, her head spinning. Hadn't she read somewhere that around sixty-five percent of pericardial effusions were sanguinous? And that around twenty-five percent of these were, in turn, caused by malignancy?

Desperation sliced through her, but it was the sharp edge of guilt that lacerated her most.

What if she'd missed something? What if it recurred? Augustin was just a kid; only eleven years old. But cardiac tamponade meant extreme pressure on his heart, preventing it from functioning properly, and next time, if his heart couldn't pump enough blood to the rest of his body, it could result in Augustin going into organ failure, and dying.

'You couldn't have seen it. And let's wait for the results before we assume the worst, shall we?' Liam's voice cut into her thoughts, as though he was reading her mind.

'How long will that take?' She didn't meant to snap at him.

But even though he hadn't levelled any criticism at her, she felt responsible that she had missed something that Liam had so easily picked up on.

In typical Liam manner, however, he didn't seem perturbed and was as cool and controlled as ever.

'Long enough for them to see whether the fluid we yielded grows mycobacteria or reveals malignant cells.'

It wasn't the answer she wanted to hear. Then again, she wasn't sure what she did want to hear. She felt itchy, somehow, and unsettled. Like her own skin was too small for her.

'You can't heal everyone with a wave of a magic wand, Talia.'

'I never thought that I could,' she scoffed, but she heard the tremor in her voice, and she knew that Liam heard it, too.

His gaze narrowed, too sharp, too astute.

'What is it?'

'Nothing,' she lied unconvincingly. Frustration bubbled through her. 'I don't know, maybe it's because Augustin is one of my kid brother's friends. They're in the same class. And his mother and mine used to be such good friends.'

'Used to be?' His forehead knitted together. 'Has Augustin lost his mother recently?'

If she could have snatched the words back and thrown them over the harbour wall and into the ocean beyond, she would have. But she'd had to open her big mouth, hadn't she? And now Liam had her pinned down with that all-seeing gaze of his.

She hated it.

*Hated.*

'Forget it, it isn't like that.' It took everything she had to force her legs into something resembling a forward motion. Faster, and faster, as she began to hurry down the corridor and away from the man who seemed to crawl under her skin no matter how tightly she'd thought she'd stitched it back up.

'Talia...?'

'I have work to do, and your shift must be over,' she ground out. 'I'm glad you were there for Augustin. I have to go.'

'Talia, wait,' he called her back and, to her eternal shame, she obeyed.

As if compelled to do exactly as he commanded.

At least she could take some comfort from the fact that he strode up the corridor towards her, meeting her halfway. But that no doubt held more significance to her than to him.

'What is it?' She forced a professional smile. At least, she hoped it was professional.

Yet when he took her arm and steered her into

an empty side room, she was powerless to stop the blood from racing through her. The door closed and she looked up at him expectantly.

She certainly wasn't prepared for the unreadable expression in his eyes.

'I was sorry to hear about your mama,' he told her quietly. Sincerely.

Talia froze, all the same.

'How did you find out about that?' she managed to ask.

'It's a hospital, you know how people talk,' he replied with a half-smile. Not exactly an apology, but closer than not.

'What did you hear?' She didn't really want to know the answer, but she felt compelled to ask all the same.

'Just that she died a couple of years ago.'

And she could have left it there. She could have breathed a sigh of relief that he didn't know anything more than that.

'Three years ago, actually,' Talia burst out before she could stop herself, as if she wanted him to finally know.

She didn't care to examine *why*.

'Three years?' He frowned, his gaze sharpening on her. 'After you'd left… Duke's?'

'*When* I left,' she stated flatly.

He stared at her, almost icily, for far too long. It was all she could do not to shift uncomfortably.

'But that isn't why you left?' he asked at last. 'Because your mother…mama had died?'

'No, but…it was a short illness.'

'You used to talk to your family every Sunday.' His frown deepened. 'You never once mentioned she wasn't well.'

She didn't realise she'd bitten her lip, hard enough to draw blood, until she tasted the faint metallic taste.

'I didn't know. She made them keep it from me because she didn't want to ruin my move to North Carolina.'

A hard ball lodged itself in her throat and she couldn't continue.

'So, what happened? They called you that last day to tell you and you jumped straight on a flight?'

'Pretty much,' she mumbled.

Even now, three years on, it still pained her to think of that day. The realisation that her mama was so ill, and the guilt. That overwhelming sense of remorse.

'I guess I'd known something was wrong for a while,' Talia heard herself confessing. 'She hadn't looked quite…*right*. And she was always so tired. I just didn't want to see it so I think I told myself it was nothing.'

His eyes glittered, a tautness shifting around his face, and something twisted inside her. She told herself that she didn't care what that *some-*

*thing* was, but deep down she knew that wasn't entirely true.

'Why didn't you tell me?' he demanded eventually.

'You were at work.'

Censure moved over his features. And something else that she didn't care to identify.

'I would have been there for you.'

'Would you?' The words slipped out unchecked. More of an accusation than a question. 'You were always about work. It came first, second and third to you. And you'd already told me about the surgeries you had that day.'

It was only later that she'd really analysed just how many of their conversations had revolved around work, patients, procedures.

Work and sex. That was all they'd had. There had certainly been no opening up to each other about themselves as individuals.

'Besides, I rarely even talked to you about my family because I was always conscious that you never talked about yours.'

'I told you about mine.' He shrugged. 'My mother died when I was younger, my father and I aren't close, and I don't have any siblings.'

'And that's it.' She threw her arms up. 'That's all I ever knew about you.'

'Because that's all there is to know.' He sounded so casual that anyone else might have believed him.

But she knew better.

'I don't believe that, Liam.' Talia shook her head. 'In all the time we were together you never shared any childhood memories. Not one. You never had any stories.'

'I'm a surgeon, Talia, not a storyteller.' His tone was as even and controlled as ever.

She gritted her teeth, deciding she'd never hated it more.

'And that's another thing you always did,' she told him. 'Whenever I tried to get to know you, you always shut me out.'

'This conversation is going nowhere,' he stated flatly.

'Of course it isn't, because you would never let that happen. But there has to be more to you than surgeries and your career, Liam.'

'Talia—'

'It's too much, Liam. No wonder I couldn't bear it that you never shared anything with me. *Never.*'

'Because I don't throw open my life for the whole world to see everything about me?'

'I'm not talking about throwing anything open, and I'm not *the whole world,*' she cried. 'I just wanted to feel like I was a part of your life, not merely a convenient warm body.'

'You were never *merely a convenient body,*' he exploded suddenly, and what did it say about her that she felt some tiny victory that she'd finally pushed his resolve enough for him to lose that famed control? 'I'm insulted that you can even accuse me of that.'

'Well, you hardly wanted to share your life with me—which was all that I ever wanted with you.'

'So much so that you didn't even contact me when you found out your mama was ill. You didn't even leave a note. You just left.'

'Don't tell me you're offended that I didn't share details of my life?' The irony of it pulled at her mouth until she felt something of a bitter smile. '*You?* Of all people?'

'So that's why you left,' Liam said scornfully. 'Because I didn't tell you all the ins and outs of my life? My past?'

'You're oversimplifying it.' She blew out a breath of frustration, as Liam looked as more distant and forbidding than ever.

'Whilst you're overdramatising it.'

She didn't miss the way he had pulled himself harshly back under control. Or was on his way to doing so, anyway. That flash of emotion had been locked away somewhere deep inside him, as he always did.

She began to remark on it but then the words stuck in her throat as a great swell of sadness washed over her. What was the point of them arguing? What did she even think that might achieve opening up old wounds?

'What is it?' He frowned.

'Never mind.'

He eyed her disparagingly.

'You've said plenty already, why stop now?'

'Because I don't want to go down this route any more,' she confessed. 'Do you?'

He looked a little taken aback but he recovered quickly.

'No,' he answered frankly. 'I do not.'

Talia nodded.

'So…where do we go from here?'

He didn't move, but she got the impression he was regrouping. Steadying himself again. And then he smiled. A reserved but genuine expression that seemed to pull at her heart.

'Your island tour the other day was something of a blast of fresh air.'

'It was,' she agreed.

It had been more than that, though. She'd felt more alive than she'd done in a while. The fact that it had been with Liam couldn't just be a co-incidence.

'So why not enjoy each other's company for the remainder of my stay? What harm could it do?'

'I'd like that,' she answered softly.

The strangest thing about it was that, having finally confessed to him about the catalyst for her leaving North Carolina, it was as though some weight had lifted.

She missed her mama, she always would, but

a part of her felt as though she'd been grieving for the past three years. Not just after losing a precious parent but having it come so closely on the heels of losing Liam, too. Or, more accurately, losing the relationship she'd imagined they might have.

But now things felt different. She felt renewed somehow, spending time with Liam and talking to him. They were almost, *almost* back to the good times that she remembered. Without the sex, of course.

And who needed sex? She swallowed hard.

The point was that this time was different. This time she was in no danger of losing her heart. They were friends, nothing more, and in another few weeks he would be gone from her island.

Why not enjoy this unexpected friendship for what it was? And for the short time it would last? But she needed something different. Something thrilling, that Liam had never tried before.

Tossing her head back, she flashed him her brightest smile.

'New plan, let's go bodyboarding.'

'Bodyboarding?'

He arched his eyebrows.

'I seem to remember taking you skiing, back in North Carolina. Your balance was shocking, or don't you remember falling off that T-bar lift and taking out the next five couples like a bowling ball knocking down pins?'

'Until some lad caught me by my hair. She winced. 'The shameful memory is imprinted into my brain for ever. I must have looked such a state.'

Liam grimaced.

'Not so much of a state that he didn't start chatting you up. I wanted to punch him to get him to take his hands off you.'

'I don't remember that.' She looked at him in surprise, trying to work out whether she was more startled by the idea of Liam sounding almost jealous or the idea of him punching anybody.

He hadn't given her the slightest indication of either at the time. She decided she couldn't even imagine the latter. The ego boost was nice, all the same.

'Well, bodyboarding is nothing like skiing,' she declared emphatically. 'I've been teaching my brothers. If you want a lesson, Liam, meet me on the beach this afternoon.'

'I don't have anything to swim in. Or a board, for that matter.'

'We can hire boards at the beach as well as surf tops for upper body protection.'

She was warming to the idea more and more. And judging by Liam's grin, he was equally taken with the idea. But, then, he had always loved his sports—it was one of the areas where they'd bonded the most.

'Okay,' he agreed. 'Which beach?'

She gave him the directions, watching him leave and trying not to feel so pleased with herself.

It was only afterwards that she considered that she didn't have her swim gear with her—unless she was planning on bodyboarding in her scrubs.

She could head home as soon as her shift finished but it was in the opposite direction from the beach, and it would be better if she could head straight there if they were going to maximise their time. There was nothing else for it, she was going to have to head to the local market on the way over.

*Unless she borrowed something.*

The thought walloped into her hard, as her mind conjured up an image of the bikini Nyla had shown her.

Was that why the beach and surfing had been in her mind?

Admittedly, the bikini was less of a swim *piece* and more of a swim *bit*.

*Did she really dare?*

She tried to imagine Liam's reaction, and then caught herself. What was she doing, imagining eliciting some reaction from an old boyfriend?

Except that Liam wasn't simply some old boyfriend. He was the only man she'd ever loved. And she was giving him a bodyboarding lesson because they were friends, and to help them in working well as colleagues. It wasn't about anything else.

As many times as she seemed to remind herself of that fact, her brain seemed determined to ignore it. How many times did she need to learn the same lessons?

Talia blew out a long breath. If she wasn't careful, she was afraid that she was more at risk of falling for Liam than ever.

# CHAPTER NINE

HE DID *NOT* like her bikini, Liam growled to himself a few hours later. Or, more accurately, he liked it rather too much.

A gloriously vibrant yellow thing with bright green floral detailing, which appeared to be little more than four triangles of fabric connected with other narrow strips of the same energising green material as the flowers.

It made that feral beast inside him roar with approval.

*Mine.*

He hadn't been able to keep his hands off Talia the other day when she'd been fully clothed. How the hell was he supposed to concentrate on his damned lesson with her looking like *that?*

So much for just trying to be friends. Apparently, it didn't matter what his brain—or logic—dictated, his body seemed hell-bent on proving otherwise. His teeth actually itched—as if they were resisting some carnal urge to rip the flimsy swim-set off, right there and then.

He watched her manoeuvre the board. So graceful, so supple. Doing little to help him clear his head of the unwanted, unhelpful images. The way they had been together. That heat. That fire. Like nobody else.

Because that was the truth of it, wasn't it?

There had never been anybody like Talia. Not before, and definitely not since. From the moment they'd met, that flame had burned within him. Hotter and brighter than anything he'd ever dreamed could exist. He'd lost himself in her more times than he'd been able to count, and the worst of it was that, deep down, he'd believed it was always going to be that way.

It was almost a relief when she stopped at the edge of the ocean and pulled on the surf top, covering a swathe of mouth-watering skin. *Almost.*

She looked up at him and flashed her trademark grin.

'Okay, put your top on, it will help protect your body, though I don't imagine you'll be riding any serious waves to result in a real wipe-out.'

Was it his imagination or was her smile even brighter—wider—than he remembered it from three years ago? Pulling on his top and heading towards her, Liam mulled the idea over.

She'd always claimed that she couldn't wait to get away from St Victoria and see the rest of the world. Yet it seemed to him that she was more relaxed here than he'd ever seen her. Happier, somehow. As though this place fitted her better than she'd claimed it had.

'Good.' Talia dragged him from his internal

ponderings. 'Now, take your board and tie the leash around your upper arm. Great, now let's practise. Lie down on the board with your stomach on the back end of the board and your hands on the nose.'

'It might be more effective to get into the water first,' he suggested dryly, but Talia only shot him a dark look.

'It's easier to practise on dry land than to try it for the first time in water. Look, I'll show you.'

She dropped the board and moved agilely into position, showcasing her athletic build and, though he tried not to stare, her peachy round backside. It occurred to him that dropping down to lie on the board might not be the worst idea in the world.

'So, when we paddle out, you'll need to move yourself further up to the centre of the board and propel it with your arms like this...'

Dutifully, Liam obeyed, fervently hoping that by concentrating he could take his mind off Talia's body and that undeniable chemistry that was once again arcing between them.

For several moments she showed him what they were going to do, and then she leapt up and grabbed her board.

'Cool, okay, let's go.'

They waded out until they were about knee-deep before she instructed him to lay his board down and try getting on it to paddle, and he couldn't help but think she was enjoying herself a little too much. As if she thought he had decided it was all too easy. But he wasn't that naïve.

Carefully, he followed her instruction, noting how she didn't take them out too far but looked for waves that were coming in as square on to the beach as possible, and he strove to do the same, only to get flipped straight over.

'Nice attempt.' Talia grinned as he resurfaced. 'Next time, try adjusting the angle of your weight on the board.'

Another attempt, another flip. But on his third go he managed to control the board all the way.

'Impressive,' she conceded, only half grudgingly, he thought. 'I knew you'd be athletic enough to pick this up quickly.'

'I'll take that as a compliment,' he shot back, privately admiring the way she managed to steer her board left and right with the surf, back arched and head high, while he barely kept in whichever line the wave carried him.

Time after time, he practised the moves, listening to her instructions and modifying his approach until he felt he'd really got the hang of it. It was certainly even more fun than he'd anticipated, though whether that was the sport, the heat or the company, he wasn't entirely sure.

'You want to try going out a little further?' she asked after about an hour. 'There are some bigger waves out there.'

'No, I think I'll go back to the beach and catch my breath.' He laughed.

He'd thought himself fit from all the swimming, skiing and running he did, but this was something else entirely. His heart was hammering with the effort of controlling the board and his body, and the sand had never looked so appealing.

Plus, he needed a moment to sort out the jumble of...*things* in his head.

'You stay out if you want,' he added, as he caught her eyeing up the bigger waves slightly wistfully.

'You're sure?'

'Absolutely.'

Picking up his board, Liam headed for the beach, only too grateful to reach the shore and detach the leash before crashing on the still-warm sand, his chest heaving slightly with the exertion.

Back out in the ocean, Talia was already duck-diving beyond the smaller waves to catch the bigger breakers, and spinning three-sixties on her board, both horizontally and vertically, all while still riding the wave. More than impressive.

He felt that familiar pull of desire and tried to shove it back down again. But he'd noticed that the more time they spend together, the more difficult it was to ignore. And he wasn't the only one apparently admiring her. He'd spotted a couple of other bodyboarders making their way over to talk to her earlier as well as some surfer, and he'd had to remind himself that who she flirted with, or even dated, was none of his business.

It hadn't been for the last three years. But that knowledge didn't seem to make him feel any less…agitated.

Flopping back onto the beach, he forced himself not to watch. Not to give in to this ugly, clawing thing inside him that he knew couldn't possibly be jealousy. A pointless, distasteful emotion that he'd always sworn would never have a role in his life. Especially seeing how it had played out in his father.

Seeing the grief at losing his wife, warring with his jealousy that their infant son—he himself—still had his life.

Liam was so wrapped up in his thoughts that he was caught completely off guard when a stream of cold water dropped mercilessly onto his stomach.

Leaping up with a low curse, he reached out and snagged a giggling Talia as she tried to dart away.

'I thought you were going to play in the big waves,' he growled.

'I was,' she sounded breathless. 'But it wasn't as much fun without you.'

He didn't answer, instead choosing to haul her closer. It was only when he felt the electric contact of skin to skin that he realised it was her surf top that she'd removed and wrung out over him.

Now she was clad only in that flimsy bit of bikini. And it was the only thing between his skin and hers as she was pressed against him.

Liam commanded himself to release her, but his body had chosen that moment to refuse to take orders. And when he looked at her, her eyes seemed to shimmer up at him as her lush body brushed gently against him. But he didn't think she was any more in control of the moment than he was.

'This can't happen,' he managed, his voice unmistakeably hoarse. 'The other night...we already agreed.'

She made a low sound at the back of her throat that could have been either an agreement or a rebuttal, with neither of them daring to move. Echoes of the way she'd come apart in his arms, only days ago, seemed to swirl on the light breeze around them.

He could still remember her intoxicating taste, and the heady way her eyes had widened, and darkened, when he'd lifted his fingers to his mouth.

All he could think of now was crushing his mouth to hers, and then pulling aside each of those scrappy triangles in turn to take each of those dark, pert nipples that the bright green and yellow dye did nothing to disguise, and lick them and suck on them until she was moving against him, crying out his name.

Just like she'd done countless times in the past.

'It makes no sense to muddy things between us.'

His mouth was millimetres from hers, her hot, sweet breath skating over his lips. Seducing him.

'None,' she murmured.

And still they stood there—perfectly still. Yet whole currents of attraction arced between them, neither of them daring to speak again.

Liam wasn't even certain that he hadn't stopped breathing.

Faintly, so very faintly, the sound of voices finally began to penetrate his consciousness, and he slowly remembered they weren't alone. Against the objections of every fibre of his being, he leisurely peeled his hand from the perfection of the small of Talia's back and took a small step away from her.

The slight downturn of her mouth was nothing in comparison to the howling going on inside his body.

He made himself take another step, though he had no idea how he managed it.

'I think your surf mates were getting ready to close up their cabin,' he managed to bite out. 'We should take the gear back to them.'

'Right.' She sounded as dazed as he felt, though he wasn't sure if that was a comfort. 'I'll take the boards back now. Do you want to gather up our other stuff?'

He bobbed his head, suddenly aware that he was in no position to go anywhere. His body was still hard, ready. For Talia. Torpedoing every lie he was trying to tell himself about their relationship. Proving that the chemistry was as dangerous as ever.

He headed for the water before he broadcast to Talia just what power she still had over him. This non-date had already stirred too much in him. He couldn't tell whether it was the holiday-style destination or the reunion with Talia, but this didn't feel like just a medical trip any more.

Perhaps it never had. Either way, something seemed to have shifted inside him. And he couldn't afford that.

He needed to get back to his hotel room and regroup before he lost control as he had done back in his office. Perhaps spending time with the woman he'd once cared so deeply for wasn't the best option after all. It seemed it was making him lose his mind.

Why else would he have to keep reminding himself how she had walked out on him without a word? Without even the slightest indication. Just like everyone else in his life had done.

But that time—with Talia—it had more than hurt. The pain had turned him inside out. Until he'd barely been able to tell who he was any longer.

It had taken him a shamefully long time to re-surface. To stop feeling as though everything he did was a battle through some dense, suffocating fug. To feel vaguely human again. Or perhaps it was more that he'd managed to stop himself *feeling* at all.

He'd even tried dating. Doomed, painful occasions that he could count on one hand—not that his dates had given any indication that they'd found it equally as laboured. They'd even hinted at second dates, which he'd been compelled to studiously avoid, without causing offence.

Because what was the point? None of them had quite been...*her.* None of them had even come close to getting under his skin the way that Talia had.

And even though he'd told himself that was *exactly* what he wanted—someone who was nothing like *her*—none of those other, perfectly lovely, women had been enough to arrest him the way that Talia had.

'What is this? A final swim?'

He swung around as he heard her splashing through the waves behind him; graceful strokes that once again put her elegant body on display. Precisely the opposite of what he was trying to achieve right now.

'Something like that,' he answered, launching

himself into the waves and setting off on a freestyle across the section from one rocky breakwater to the next.

A punishing pace designed to occupy his body *and* mind.

Everything had changed since he'd come to St Victoria—Talia's home island. Her presence was threatening to turn everything upside down again and he couldn't seem to stop her because, despite everything, God help him, it seemed he wanted her as much as ever.

In the physical sense, anyway. This unfinished business was about the hunger that still gnawed at them both. It had been in their kiss on that first day, and he'd seen it in her eyes back in the marketplace. It was in the way her breath caught, matching the hitch of his chest as if they were in perfect harmony.

She wanted him just as badly as he wanted her. That *thing* between them had always been so primitive, so feral that it had always seemed to have a life of its own.

It had wound its way through them, binding them together. Hadn't he learned in basic chemistry—back in that boarding school that had seemed like bliss compared to any semblance of *home life* his father could have offered—that heat, oxygen and fuel were all the necessary ingredients for a perfect fire triangle?

Take away any one of them and the fire died.

The problem with he and Talia had been that the flame had never had a chance to die out by itself—naturally—the way it surely would have done in time. They'd parted way too early, and that was surely what made this attraction all the more compelling now. They hadn't given it long enough for the passion to exhaust itself and fade away by itself.

So was this Fate giving him another chance? Not just bringing him to The Island Clinic to run a highly coveted medical case, but also a last opportunity for him to indulge in Talia until they were both—finally—well and truly sated.

Until there was nothing left between them?

Until he finally got his *closure*?

This wasn't about renewing anything with Talia, or picking up their life together where they'd left off—they'd both agreed that wouldn't work. This was about the physical connection. Pure and simple. It was about glutting themselves until there was nothing left. Only then could they finally each go their separate ways without that weighted tether of unfinished business.

As if to emphasise the rightness of his decision, the ocean chose that moment to lift up another huge wave and slam Talia back into him. And if he took the opportunity to manoeuvre himself just a little more directly into its path, to catch her against him, surely that was of no interest to anybody else?

Before she had chance to pull away again he wrapped her legs around his waist and hauled her to him. Not close enough to touch. Not quite. But close enough to feel her heat. And close enough for all that delicious *need* to pool between them.

She braced her hands on his shoulders but neither pushed him away nor pulled him closer, as if she was engaging in an internal battle as fierce as his own had been moments earlier. And when she finally spoke, her voice caught in her throat; breathier, hoarser than he knew she would have preferred.

A lick of triumph ran through him. Almost visceral.

'What are you doing, Liam?'

'Such a redundant question,' he murmured, letting his words skim her silky, wet shoulders while taking care to hold himself still and not to move against her, even as every fibre of his being ached to do that.

Giving her chance to… He didn't know what.

'You made it abundantly clear to me that you didn't want this.'

Her voice sounded thick, choked. He found he rather liked it.

'I think we both know we want this,' he murmured. 'We just don't *want* to want it. But maybe I'm tired of fighting. Maybe I just want to give in to it for once.'

'Maybe I want that, too,' she breathed.

And, still, she didn't move. If anything, Liam fancied that she held herself impressively still, as if to avoid breaking the perceived fragility of the moment.

For several long moments neither of them spoke. The only sounds were those of the birds flying overhead and the water *shushing* onto the shore behind them.

And still he resisted the waves' movements as they rocked Talia's luscious body against his. Her breasts, as full and perfect as he remembered, brushed tantalising over his chest, but he refused to allow contact any lower. Not yet. Though it was nearly killing him not to do so.

'I want to hear the words, Talia,' he growled eventually. 'After the other night, I find I need to hear you *say* that you want it.'

'Is that so?' she muttered.

He felt frayed. His self-control shredded. Reaching out, he wound a coil of deep black hair around his finger and tugged gently. A tiny gesture he didn't like to admit he'd missed over the past three years. Her sigh was involuntary and instantaneous.

Liam reached for another glorious curl, taking his time. Playing with her. Toying, one might say. She was getting as tightly wound as his hair around her finger, he could feel it in every roll of her body.

With a careful movement, he allowed one hand to sweep over her. Down that uncommonly toned, impossibly soft, expanse of back that he could picture as though even through his very fingertips.

'Liam…' she sighed.

'The words, Talia.'

Trailing lower, he grazed over the delectable curve of her backside, skirting the flimsy fabric as though his fingers might just, possibly, inch beneath. He didn't know who he was tormenting more, Talia or himself.

Lord, how much had he had missed the way her eyes darkened as they locked with his; and the faint parting of her lips as her breath escaped, ragged and torn?

Even now she flicked her tongue out over her lips, as effective as a lick over the hardest part of his body.

'If we don't get out of the ocean soon, I think we might end up giving people a show,' she whispered.

'The words, Talia.' His voice scraped through him, and as much as he hated that he was revealing so much, he was helpless to prevent it.

'You're impossible,' she managed at last, and

he revelled in the undiluted surrender in her tone. 'Fine, I want this. *You.* Are you happy now?'

'Ecstatic,' he growled, pulling her right up against him and slamming his mouth into hers.

Because whatever else he told himself, he'd been dreaming of her—intimately—ever since that first day in his office. Every fantasy hotter than the last—yet not a single one of them matching up to how she truly felt in reality.

The way her lips parted for him, her head angling for a deeper fit.

He ran his hands over her again, glorying in the way she moulded herself to his touch. Matching him as naturally as ever. Somehow, still—even he wasn't even sure how he kept his resolve—maintaining that tiny pocket between them where her heat would otherwise have met his need.

As if it had only been yesterday, and not three years ago, that she'd left his presence for good. As if all that torment had been little more than some dreadful phantasm. As if she'd never broken him at all.

*Enough.*

Abruptly, he released her, dropping her lightly into the ocean and letting the water swirl all that heat, all those memories away. They didn't belong in this new scenario and he had no intention of letting them hop along for the ride.

'Let's go.'

Her breathing was shallow and fast, and the beast in him revelled in that fact.

'Where?'

'My hotel room,' he barked out. 'Any objections?'

'Not exactly.' And there it was…that hint of mischief he loved so much. 'In fact, I thought you'd never ask.'

# CHAPTER TEN

IT HAD TO be the longest walk from the beach to find a taxi, with neither of them wanting to speak or to break the spell that seemed to entwine them. Not an awkward silence but more a laden one, heavy with anticipation.

Then they slid into the taxi, Liam's leg pressed tightly against hers, searing her where she sat, yet both of them fighting every primitive urge to touch anywhere else lest they found themselves unable to keep their hands off each other.

The back of a taxi was certainly not the ideal setting, the audience even less so.

The journey seemed to take an eternity. With every second that delicious fraught, charged need between them cranked up another notch. Then another.

But finally they arrived, the stunning Island Clinic's hotel, a more than welcome sight. It was all Talia could do not to tumble out of the taxi, but she was gratified when Liam, having shoved more than enough money at their driver with a hasty word of thanks, grabbed her hand and hurried them both through the lobby and into the elevator.

His arm was snaking around her waist even as the doors pinged closed, hauling her to him and claiming her mouth with his own as if he couldn't wait a moment longer.

She knew she couldn't.

Looping her hands around his neck, Talia pulled her body as close to him as possible, moulding herself to him so that there wasn't a spare millimetre of space between them. But it still wasn't close enough.

He plundered her mouth with his tongue, thrilling and daring, and it felt like both a promise and warning of what was to come. He kissed her until the roaring in her ears felt almost deafening, and then he blazed a trail all the way across her jaw and down the line of her neck, stopping only to offer extra special consideration to that sensitive hollow by her collarbone.

How had she forgotten quite what that talented mouth could do to her? Even in the fantasies she'd like to pretend she didn't have, the memories she'd replayed like old, X-rated movies, she had somehow downplayed the incredible effect he had on her.

It was a wrench when he tore his mouth from hers as the elevator finally slowed, and Talia felt almost ridiculously grateful when he took her hand once again, striding down the corridor and sliding his key card against the room lock.

And then, *at last*, they were inside. The door closed tightly. Alone.

'Next time,' Liam managed gruffly, sweeping her against him again, 'we don't go so far from the hotel.'

'Less talking, more kissing,' she muttered, pressing her lips to his and pouring herself back into the moment.

Because she wanted him more than she could ever remember wanting—*needing*—anything. And what was the point of thinking any further outside that simple truth? As soon as Liam's case at the clinic was complete he would be gone, and she would still be with her family where she was most needed. So she had nothing to lose.

*Right?*

Dragging her mouth from his, she began languidly unhooking the first button of his shirt, the second, the third, deliberately taking her time and giving it her full attention, until the two sides fell away in front of her. It was worth the wait, exposing all those mouth-wateringly hard ridges that made her hands ache to touch and her lips yearn to kiss.

She bent her head as if to do just that but Liam, it seemed, had other plans. Hooking her legs around his waist, just as he had done in the sea what seemed like a lifetime ago, he manoeuvred them both until her back was pressed against the wall, his hardness pressed into her heat.

He breathed in sharply, and she heard a low carnal groan of pleasure that took her a moment to realise was her. Three years of missing him—and pretending that she wasn't—and suddenly here they were. She didn't want to wait any longer.

Rolling her hips, she pressed herself against him again, revelling in the way he inhaled again. Even sharper this time. He afforded her another intense look, his green eyes almost black, but he didn't move.

'Forgotten what to do?' she teased, her own voice sounding gravelly in her ear.

'Oh, trust me, I haven't forgotten a thing,' he gritted out, and it rasped over her skin, leaving a trail of goose-bumps in its wake. 'Just giving you chance to change your mind.'

Desire fired anew along her veins. She shook her mind, her voice almost deserting her for a moment.

'I have no intention of changing my mind. I want this, Liam.'

She just about managed to slam her mouth shut before she added, *I want you.*

'Good,' he replied, and for a fraction of a moment she wondered what he was replying to.

Then, without another word, he swung her—legs still wrapped around his hips—around and carried her across the threshold to the huge bed that dominated the other room. And then she was sprawled on the bed as he concerned himself with stripping her very efficiently and very thoroughly until the only thing that remained between them was a tiny triangle of emerald-green lace.

Her heart thudded loudly in her ears. Like the downdraught from the celebrity helicopters that landed so frequently on the helipad at The Island Clinic—only ten times louder. And harder.

She felt wild. Incredible. The best she'd felt in three years. Or longer. Because he'd never quite looked at her the way he was looking at her now—as if that invisible cage that he pretended didn't confine him back at Duke's no longer existed.

Abruptly, she realised that he'd been looking more and more relaxed with each passing day here on St Vic and she opened her mouth to tell him, before abruptly snapping it shut again.

Now definitely wasn't the best time to tell him.

'Some other clever quip you thought better of?' he demanded, a smiled twisting one side of his mouth.

Talia forced a smile of her own.

'Something like that.'

'Then allow me to disabuse you of any more of them,' he growled, before sinking to his knees, sliding his hands under her backside and using

those powerful shoulders of his to part her legs
a little further.

And then, in a sublime flash of colour and
heat, he buried his face between her legs and
Talia forgot anything else.

The flimsy fabric was gone in a second and,
*Lord*, if she didn't taste even more incredible than
he remembered. Caramel and cream, hot and perfect on his tongue. Liam drank her in deeply. *His*
Talia. A woman wholly unlike any other.

Three years had done nothing to diminish the
compulsion he'd felt for her. The other day had
been little more than an appetiser and he'd been
on tenterhooks ever since. Now he had her back
again—if only temporarily—he intended to indulge in every last second.

He licked around her, his tongue and fingers
in harmony as he played with her, teased her.
She was so very slick, and hot, and he revelled
in the way she gasped and writhed beneath his
touch. The way she arched her body that moved
those perfect breasts tipped with obsidian, and
the way she rolled her hips towards him as if she
couldn't stop herself from trying to get closer to
his mouth.

Those feral sounds she was making at the back
of her throat did little to ease his arousal, so hard
that it was almost painful. But Liam ignored it.

This moment was about Talia's need, not his. Not yet. After all, they had all night.

He licked deeper, letting his voice rumble and vibrate against the very centre of her need as he let her know just how remarkable she was. He basked in the sensation of her hands reaching for him, her fingers biting into his shoulders.

Her moans were becoming louder now, more insistent. Each one jolted through him like flashes of spectacular lightning.

How he'd missed this. *Her*. Her sound, her scent, her taste. It made him ache again and, this time, he couldn't take any more. Moving his mouth that final millimetre, to the very centre of her core, he found what he was looking for and sucked. Hard.

Talia screamed. A low, glorious sound that seemed to echo all around him. Her grip tightened on his shoulders as she bucked wildly at his mouth, but he held her backside and licked all the more. Again and again, she shattered beneath him and it occurred to him that surely he had never seen her as beautiful as she was now.

The woman he'd thought he'd lost—and perhaps he had—but he had her back now. If only for a single month. He might not be able to offer her the marriage or the family that she wanted, but since she hadn't yet found it with someone more worthy then he could offer her one final, perfect month.

'Aren't you overdressed?' Talia panted when she finally came back to herself, as if it had suddenly occurred to her that she was the only one fully undressed.

He liked the fact that it had taken her quite a time. And he also liked the slight flush of colour he could detect in her cheeks. Exertion? Embarrassment at her abandon? Or both?

'If you want me undressed, you only have to ask,' he remarked dryly.

She narrowed her eyes at him, flipping herself into a sitting position before he realised what she was doing. That suppleness, litheness that he'd always admired. Reaching out with her hand, she caught him by the waist of his cargo shorts, and pulled him closer, her eyes locking with his.

'Who said anything about asking?'

The husky tone threaded its way around the room, and right through Liam. It coiled low in his abdomen.

And lower again.

He couldn't pull his gaze away for a second, her rich brown eyes captivating him as she stared at him; a gleam telling that she knew precisely what she was doing with every slow pull of the zipper. Right over where he was hardest for her.

The sight of her mouth, right there, so close to

him, was almost too hard to handle. And then she flicked her tongue over her lips as if she knew exactly what he was thinking. *Dear God*, if she did that, he feared he might embarrass himself right there and then.

'Not yet,' he growled out, pulling away from her.

'Why not?' It was more of a challenge than a question. His Talia had never been a shrinking violet, either in bed or out of it. It was one of the things that he admired most about her.

She was stunning. Incredible. She had haunted his dreams but he hadn't expected to ever see her again in the flesh. Then he'd received that call; discovered that she was the one who had put his name forward. And now they were here, and she was real; and he'd be damned if he'd let things go off like that. With him in her mouth.

Stripping off the rest of his clothes, he pushed her gently back on the bed and nudged her legs apart again with his knee.

'Stop asking questions and just kiss me,' he ordered instead, nonetheless with a thread of surprise when she sighed softly, looped her arms over his neck and simply complied.

He had no idea how long they kissed, lost in the glory of each other. He relearned every inch of her delectable body from the long, elegant line of her neck to the exquisite swell of her chest.

He took one nipple in his mouth, lavishing

such care and attention on it that he thought he might burst from his own need, then he turned his focus to the other. He traced the dip at the side of her waist and drew whorls with his fingers and his tongue, all the way to her belly button, and the ring that he remembered nestling in there.

'This all feels rather…one-sided,' she breathed at one point.

He could barely make his voice work long enough to assure her that it wasn't. It wasn't at all.

And it wasn't just about rediscovering her body, the hazy realisation crept through Liam's mind at one point. It also felt as though he had found where Talia had been hiding all this time. He just had no idea what he was supposed to be doing with such a discovery.

She shifted abruptly, and he wasn't ready for it. All of a sudden he found himself nestled at her entrance. His blunt head against all that wet heat, and he couldn't run any more. Even if he'd thought to, Talia suddenly slid her hands down his back, raised her hips, and drew him straight inside her.

He groaned as she swivelled her hips, drawing him as deep as she could. So deep that as he scooped her to him and began to move, he couldn't be sure where one of them ended and the other began.

She clung to him, her hips moving to his rhythm and meeting him stroke for stroke. With his free hand, he allowed himself to roam her body, caressing her velvety skin, his mouth pressed against that hollow that he knew sent her wild.

Her gasps and moans were like a song, swelling in his chest. He slid out of her, then back in, and the song grew louder. He moved again, then again, and again, the pace becoming more and more devastating each time. A wildfire that was growing too much to contain.

He ran his hand down the front of her body, feeling the way her body rippled beneath him, until he reached between them right to where her body knew its desire, driving her to the edge. Closer and closer, until he could barely hold his own control any longer.

And this time when she went catapulting upwards, soaring into some blissful oblivion and sobbing his name, Liam finally let himself follow her.

# CHAPTER ELEVEN

*IT HAD DEFINITELY been about revenge,* Talia decided several days later as she ushered her patient gently out of one of the St Vic's Hospital's dressings rooms and began cleaning it down before she could call the next patient through.

She'd been aching for him ever since their night together. Practically climbing out of her own skin every time she replayed it, but helpless to do anything. He'd reached for her again and again during that perfect night, but when she'd finally woken the next day—sated and deliciously sore in places she'd forgotten even existed—he'd been gone. Called back to surgeries, the way he always had been.

They hadn't talked. Or, at least, about nothing of any consequence. It had been more than apparent that it had been about a physical union, but not an emotional one. She shouldn't have been surprised. But even so, since then she'd spent every moment snapping her head around every time someone walked around a corner, just to see if it was him.

It never was.

Now that he had what he wanted, was that supposed to be it? Hardly the Liam she'd known... but, then, they both knew where that had got them.

Talia sprayed down the plastic chair, almost angrily, and began to vigorously swipe at it. The problem wasn't what that night *was,* she decided crossly, as much as what it *wasn't.* She'd wanted the sex, yes, but she'd also been foolish enough to want more. Naïve enough to think that emotions might follow. Even though they never had before.

She wanted *more.*

Maybe she shouldn't have given in to the temptation that was Liam Miller. That bikini might not have been her best idea, though she hardly doubted that what she wore had anything to do with how much he desired her. It was gratifying to know that he'd wanted her just as badly that first day dressed in her scrubs.

And so what if he wasn't offering anything more than a month-long booty call? She could handle it. She wasn't the naïve girl she'd been three years ago, and she wasn't in a position to look for a relationship any longer.

Not that she *wanted* a relationship, she reminded herself hastily. There was still too much to resolve here with her brothers and her father before she could start thinking about herself.

Nonetheless, every night she played her own private home movie of their time together. If she'd thought it had been bad over the last few years, it was nothing compared to the wealth of sensation he'd unleashed in her since the day in the ocean.

The worst of it was that she could now recall every single intimate moment with Liam in brilliant, graphic detail. Every kiss, every taste and every last damn carnal sound.

So the fact that Liam had her constantly on the precipice of thrilled, nervous excitement, while he hadn't made contact even once during the past few days, was nothing short of *revenge.*

Hurling the wipe in the bin with unnecessary force, Talia eyed her dressings room with satisfaction. Time to stop thinking about Liam, she concluded firmly as she headed to the main desk to collect her next patient's notes.

'This is looking so much better, May.' Talia smiled approvingly as she carefully peeled back the dressing on a patient she'd been getting to know over the past few days.

'So no more honey?' the older lady asked.

'You still need the honey gauze.' Talia shook her head. 'It acts as both a cleaner and a feeder and is great for the kind of burn you have. But I think we can leave it a little longer between changes this time. What about three days this time?'

Her patient didn't look impressed, and Talia could understand it. The woman had to catch two buses to get the hospital every other day. It couldn't be easy for her. But meticulous debridement of the wound would prevent any infections from taking hold, and the honey dressing with its anti-inflammatory, anti-bacterial, antioxidant properties seemed to be working especially well.

'As long as we keep it clean and cleared out, it should only be for a little longer,' Talia encouraged. 'But if any infection got in there...'

'I know, I know.' The older woman waved her hands to cut her off. 'Three days, okay?'

'Good.'

Flashing her the kind of smile a satisfied teacher might bestow on a petulant child, Talia busied herself with cleaning the wound before cutting a small, fresh rectangle of gauze, then folding it up to place inside the wide but shallow wound.

Five minutes later and she had another satisfied—relatively—patient. Even so, as she opened the door to let the lady leave, Talia flashed her a bright, almost breezy smile.

'Don't worry about forgetting to go to the appointment desk. I'll book the appointment for you from here.'

'There's no need for that—' the older lady began, but Talia wasn't fooled.

'I know, but I'm sure you don't want me turning up at your house again.'

The only response was a grunt, and Talia smiled to herself. It was odd, the way working back here, back *home*, made her feel these days. So different from the way she'd felt three years ago.

Perhaps, if she hadn't been so blind, so pig-headed…but, no, it was pointless hanging off the *what-ifs*.

'Do you make house visits to all your patients, then?'

Talia swung around, but it was too late. Her body was already reacting, sparking, just from the sound of his voice.

She fought to rein it in and sound composed, was impressed when she even heard a bit of sass in her own voice.

'Only when they're an eighty-year-old woman who doesn't book an appointment when I tell them to.'

'I didn't realise you were so dedicated.'

She glowered at him without realising it, and was gratified when he looked instantly remorseful.

'I take that back. Of course I've always known you were dedicated, I remember several times how you rang up to check on patients who you didn't think were taking proper care of themselves. I just meant I didn't realise that you actually turned up at people's homes.'

'I couldn't in North Carolina, I would probably have been arrested for harassment, or stalking, or something. But this is St Vic, we look after each other.'

Yet another reason why this place wasn't as bad as she'd once felt it to be. And another nail of shame for her coffin of guilt.

'What is it?'

Talia didn't realise that Liam had closed the gap between them until she felt his hand on her shoulder. Worse was that look of concern on his face that made her want to break down and tell him everything. About her mother, her father, the lot.

She considered herself fortunate that pride re-asserted itself just in time. Flashing him a beam so bright that it made her face literally ache, she forced out a light laugh.

'It's absolutely nothing. What are you doing here, anyway?'

He eyed her closely, but then he abruptly filed away whatever else he might have been going to say and suddenly she knew what he was going to say.

Her entire body started to fizz in anticipation—like she was some kind of teenager on a first date again.

'I'm taking you out for a meal. You can choose the restaurant.'

'I'm working,' she told him primly, perhaps as some kind of payback for making her stew, alone, for so many days.

'Your shift ended forty-five minutes ago,' he replied evenly. 'I know, because I've been waiting outside for the last hour.'

*Oh.*

'Oh.'

She tried not to grin, but it was an effort. Especially when he told her he'd leave her to change but that he'd be waiting at what passed for Reception, and that he hadn't eaten since breakfast.

She didn't know why that should make her feel so special. Like he'd spent the entire day waiting for this moment. Like she wasn't just an afterthought. It was all she could do to take her time heading to the locker room, showering and changing.

Throwing on her clothes and skipping through the hospital would only make her look too eager.

But soon enough they were walking out of the doors, her arm linked through his in a way they'd never done at Duke's, so that all their colleagues could see they were together and Talia revelled, for the first time ever, in how that felt.

'So, where are we heading?'

'A little restaurant called Auntie Zinia's. It's homely but it's good. I think you'll like it.'

At least, she hoped he would.


'This place reminds me of The Coals House, back in North Carolina,' Liam told her, as he finished up the last mouthful of his Auntie's Curry, with its island spices, coconut milk, almonds and cashew nuts. 'Only the food is even better.'

'Yeah, I always used to feel a little bit of home whenever we ate there.' She smiled warmly. 'And you remember those orange and blue cocktails? Dream Fusions, were they called? Either way, they were lethal.'

'You missed St Victoria.' He shook his head, as if ignoring her attempt to distract him. 'You used to tell me how much you'd always wanted to get away, and I took it at face value. I don't know why I never considered you might still miss it.'

She shrugged, looking around at the old but loved décor, and the happy patrons who were more like family than customers.

'I think it maybe took being away for me to realise how much I really loved this place.'

'And your mama?'

'I think she knew how I would end up feeling. I like to think that's why she encouraged me to go. They say if you love something then you should let it go free. If it comes back to you...'

She tailed off, unable to finish.

She'd returned to St Victoria, her mama, almost too late. But, in the process she'd felt as though she'd lost Liam.

It had taken her years to accept that, like the old saying, he'd never come back to her so he'd never really been hers to begin with. But now he was here and in an odd way it was to reverse all the steps she'd made these past few years. She loved this place, and coming home had been the best decision. Yet if Liam asked her to return to North Carolina with him…would she?

She shook her head, irked by her own thoughts. This wasn't a real date. They were only enjoying each other's company for the time that he was on the island but he was never going to ask her to return with him. He was only here for one case, and after that he would be returning to Duke's alone.

So why spoil a pleasant evening with thoughts of what could never be? Shaking everything from her mind, she tilted her head to one side.

'What is it you want to know?' he asked, almost amused.

'Who says I want to know anything?'

'You always do that with your head.' He demonstrated. 'And you twirl your thumbs around each other, faster and faster the more agitated you are.'

She didn't need to glance down to check, although surreptitiously she tried to stop circling them.

'So, go on, what did you want to ask?'

She pulled a rueful face.

'I just wondered why it took so long to ask me on this date,' she asked eventually. 'Especially after what happened the other night.'

He'd spent the evening—the last few days—trying not to think about what had happened in the ocean the other day. And afterwards, of course. Not that he'd succeeded. The memory of their bodies entwined, him buried so deep inside her that he'd had no idea where she'd ended and he'd begun, had been too much to push aside.

'Why?' He schooled himself to stay calm. 'Did you think I'd forgotten?'

'No, but I began to wonder if you were drawing it out deliberately. Or think maybe it was some kind of ploy.'

'Is that right?' He let out a low, incredulous laugh, trying not to let his gaze linger too long on her body as she shifted in her seat. 'It's hardly flattering, how little you think of me, Talia. But, no, for the record, it wasn't a ploy.'

'Then why?'

'Sometimes I forget how tenacious you were. *Are.*'

'That's funny, because I never forget how quick you can be to divert conversations, particularly if they veer near the personal.'

Dragging his eyes up, he forced himself to accept the criticism, as much as he might have wanted to deny it.

'Fine,' he conceded after a moment. 'You really want to know why I waited until tonight?'

'I do.'

'I wanted it to be…right. Not rushed. Not just another night of sex—although I have to confess I'm more than open to that possibility too. But I knew you had a day off tomorrow, as do I, and I thought it would be nice to take the evening to have a meal, and talk, without either one of us having to rush off for work the next day.'

'Ah.' She looked vaguely sheepish before another expression clouded her eyes. A decidedly naughtier expression that he remembered from three years ago. 'Just to have a meal and talk?'

'Talia...' This conversation was hardly helping him keep his libido in check.

Talia had always found it far too easy to affect him like this. He wondered if she'd ever realised it.

'Only I understood this was about giving in to that attraction between us. No romance, no dating. And what you're describing sounds lovely and all, but it also sounds an awful lot like the latter.'

'What would you have preferred, Talia?' he asked, struggling to keep his tone light. 'A text instructing you to come straight to my hotel after your shift finished for a quick booty call?'

'Isn't that what the other night was about?'

'Whatever I say here, I'm damned, aren't I?' he acknowledged wryly. 'I wanted to take you out on a date. But what can I say, Talia? If you just wanted the sex, what do you think I'd have said? At the end of the day you're a stunning woman and I'm still a red-blooded male.'

She eyed him for a moment before dropping her head back and letting out a clear, slightly wicked laugh that licked up his sex as surely as if she'd been using her tongue.

'Good to know…' She lifted one smooth, bare shoulder, then dropped it. 'So why are we sitting here discussing dessert when there are far more tempting choices on the menu?'

Her eyes gleamed mischievously, and Liam found himself struggling to clear his suddenly parched throat.

'You want to leave?'

An impish smile tugged at the corners of her mouth as she made a show of smoothing down her sundress.

'I thought you'd never ask.'

He should have resisted. He wanted to. At least a part of him wanted to—the logical, rational part of his brain.

Sadly, right now he realised that his brain wasn't the bit of his anatomy that appeared to be in control. Not when a woman like Talia was casting him such decidedly wicked glances.

Forget the *woman like*. Only Talia could unbalance him like this.

He paid the bill as quickly as he could without his haste appearing unseemly, and then he slid his hand to the small hollow of her back—a gesture which she'd always loved—and guided her outside.

The joyful sounds of a street party slammed into them both, as did a swell of undulating bodies.

'Down this way.' Talia laughed, grabbing his hand and pulling him down a narrow street.

'A shortcut?'

'Geographically, it's the long way round...' she laughed again '...but tonight, yes, it's a shortcut.'

'The parade would be that difficult to navigate?'

She looked suddenly sheepish.

'That, and the fact that my brothers are in there somewhere. Fate means they would inevitably spot me with you.'

'And that's a problem because...?'

She only hesitated for a fraction of a moment, but he didn't miss it.

'Because they've only just forgiven me for not being there earlier for Mama. If they see you and me together, knowing you're from Duke's too, they might start...jumping to conclusions.'

Did she mean they blamed him for Talia not being in St Victoria?

Why wasn't he surprised? His father was right, he seemed to ruin everyone who got close to him. Except for his patients, and surgery of course. That was the only thing he had ever really had.

But he thrust that aside for now. *Just for to-*

*night*, he told himself as they moved quickly down the cobbled alleys, ducking washing and dodging kids playing football. Even getting an odd look from an elderly woman sewing and overseeing her grandchildren from her chair in a nearby doorway.

'Didn't you say that your grandmother used to get you to read to her? And that she taught you to cook?'

He didn't even know where the question had come from—possibly from talk of her family— and by the look on Talia's face, she hadn't expected him to remember either.

Even so, her expression of surprise quickly gave way to fondness.

'She still teaches me to cook.' Talia smiled. 'She says that no one can make that kitchen sing the way that she can. And she's right.'

'I seem to recall you cooked some incredible food when we were together,' he couldn't help himself saying.

'Well, if you meet Gramma, don't tell her that.' Talia chuckled. 'She'll probably try to beat you with the soft end of a sweeping brush. Actually, one look at you and she probably wouldn't. Anyway, she used to let me sit on a stool and try the batter. Though she always said that a good gramma lets her grandchild lick the beaters, but a great gramma turns them off first.'

'My grandmother taught me how to bake too.'

The detail slipped out without warning, and Talia almost tripped over the cobbles in her shock.

He caught her, wondering what the hell he was doing.

'Did she?' Talia asked, and he knew she was trying to sound casual.

Another time it might have made him smile but he was too busy trying to silence his uncharacteristic thoughts. They were still moving along the narrow streets but their pace had slowed considerably.

'Her favourite was walnut cake.'

'You made me that once,' Talia gasped.

'Did I?' He shrugged as though he didn't recall it but the memory was shamefully clear.

It had been near the end of their relationship, about a week before she'd walked out without a word.

'You just never mentioned who taught you how to bake it.'

He could see that she didn't mean to push him. She looked almost thrilled and terrified all at once and he could understand why.

Three years ago there was no way he would have ever confided anything so personal to her. To anyone. He'd barely been able to show her the box that contained painful photos of his mother. Certainly nothing else it kept so secure inside it.

He didn't know why he was opening up now. It was as though he couldn't shut himself up.

He could only put it down to the odd spell this enchanting island had been weaving around him ever since that first, stunning view from his plane.

They popped out of the warren of streets just by a taxi office, the taxi itself fortuitously parked outside.

'What else do you remember about her?' Talia pressed gently as they slid into the battered back seat.

'I don't remember her that well,' Liam heard himself say, though he couldn't have identified where the memories ever came from.

They were always little more than fuzzy images swimming in the recesses of his brain. Or a sparse jigsaw box of partial pictures. Snippets of conversation.

'Her name was Gloria, but people called her Glory.' Something new swam past his consciousness and he grasped at it. 'I think I called her… Glammy?'

He fought to focus but it was like dredging a memory up from a muddy, silty riverbed. It might have had form, but he couldn't quite be sure. He thought back to Talia and her grandmother, and something else clicked awkwardly into place.

'I think… I think I remember her giving me the beaters when she'd mixed something.'

'So she was kind?' Talia asked cautiously.

A flash of a silver-grey bob laughing over him,

perhaps? Gnarled hands smoothing hair from his forehead? Fleeting, and hazy. Maybe not even real at all.

And yet…he'd always felt as though they were. And now he found that he wanted to say that he thought she had loved him. But how could he know that?

'I think so. I used to think she loved me. But then…she went away.'

He didn't say die. He didn't think that was what had happened. He seemed to recall arguments on the phone with his father when he'd used her name. It had always made him believe that she was his maternal grandmother rather than his paternal one. And it was what had left him with a bitter taste in his mouth that she, too, had ultimately abandoned him.

If she had once loved him, it hadn't been enough.

Not that it deterred Talia. He knew why. She'd had such a happy childhood, despite the lack of money, that she hadn't been able to understand the relationship between himself and his father. She wanted him to have what she'd had.

'Is it possible you suppressed the memory?' she mused, oblivious to his internal ramblings. 'Maybe it hurt too much. Do you remember what happened to her?'

He opened his mouth to tell her that not everybody's families could be like hers, then closed it again. Why destroy her moment of hope? Hadn't he already damaged her enough?

'Not for certain.' He probed his brain to remember whatever tiny fragments were there.

And it was odd, but now he knew something was there those tiny shards were coming back to him, the tiniest sliver at a time.

'I think we might have gone to her funeral.'

Although not when she'd initially disappeared from his life. But perhaps a few years later. Was that the image he always remembered? He'd always assumed that snapshot he had of his mother's funeral had been something he'd created in his mind based on his father's description of his mother's funeral. Perhaps a photograph?

But perhaps it was actually a real memory, his own memory. Not of his mother's funeral, of course, but from his grandmother's funeral that he had actually attended?

Somewhere in the back of his mind he'd always thought he could hear a voice. A woman's voice, telling him how much his mother had loved being pregnant. How much she'd wanted to be a mom. He'd always wondered if that had been her—his grandmother.

But he couldn't be sure. And what was the point in guessing?

'If she did, I can't even remember it. I certainly don't feel it,' he ground out at last, shoving aside the uninvited feelings that were currently, suddenly, threatening everything he'd ever believed to be true.

All because of Talia. He thought it was that, perhaps, that angered him the most. This was why he should never have let things get so far—so intimate—between them.

The taxi pulled up outside The Island Clinic's luxury hotel, though he'd barely even registered the journey. He should put Talia back in the cab and send her home. But then she slid her hand into his and he forgot to do anything but walk with her.

'Liam—'

'The point is that you can now see why I really am not capable of loving you the way you want to be love,' he gritted out.

They were still moving in the direction of his suite and even though his brain was roaring that this was no longer the time, his body seemed quite content to go along with it.

'That's what you said the other day,' she pointed out evenly.

'And, dammit, Talia, it's no less true now. Why do you insist on thinking better of me than I really am?'

'And why do you insist on thinking worse?' she asked softly. 'You keep saying that you aren't capable of love but I think you're more than capable.'

'Then you're a fool,' he told her, but it lacked any real heat.

And Talia just smiled at him, gentle and encouraging.

How the hell had they got to his hotel suite?

'I think you repressed that memory, though I don't pretend to know why. It has always been there, buried, just waiting for the moment when you would start to dig it out.'

'You're wrong.'

He had been wrong to let her get so close.

'I'm not.' She smiled at him, a too-bright smile that seemed to pierce through every defence he tried to erect between them. 'But enough of that now. I didn't bring you this way to make you walk down paths you aren't ready for. I just wanted a quick way to the hotel room.'

'Talia…'

As quickly as he was trying to put up the blocks, she was tearing them down. Coming up to him and looping her arms around his neck as she wielded her body like a weapon against him.

The most effective weapon he'd ever known.

And when she pressed her soft breasts, with the taut nipples, against his chest, letting her lips brush against his, Liam let her.

After all, he was only a man, and not always a good one, at that. And then he saw the shimmering in her eyes and automatically he held his arms out for her to go to him; drawing her into his embrace as if he was a different man.

Scooping her into his arms, he carried her across the room, laying her down almost reverently on the bed, before he began stripping her. Taking his time and turning the whole thing into some elaborate show that seemed to have Talia as transfixed as he felt.

Her shoes came off first, followed by her flirty skirt, then her cropped tee, and the removal of each garment was punctuated by long, hot kisses as he reacquainted himself with every swell and every hollow.

As if the more tenderness he showed, the better he could protect her from whatever demons were loose inside himself.

# CHAPTER TWELVE

TALIA HELD HER breath as Liam gowned up, ready to operate on little Lucy Wells. And once he made his first incision—a four-centimetre incision in the midclavicular line—the procedure would finally be underway.

The past few days had been more like a dream than anything else. Pure bliss. The workplace had been harmonious, even sharing a few cases both in The Island Clinic, as well as at St Vic hospital. And when they'd been alone again, she'd lost count of the number of times he'd reached for her, and still that feeling of being sated had only lasted a short time before she'd found herself craving him again.

*Like an itch she couldn't quite scratch*, she thought, grinning to herself as she imagined his aghast reaction if she ever dared to use that expression with him.

Perhaps she should, just for fun.

It was as though that moment in the alley when he had finally, shockingly, let her into a tiny part of his past had brought them closer. As she'd always hoped it might.

Was it too much to hope that his barriers

were at last beginning to, if not crumble, at least soften? And she didn't know if it was the years that had passed, or the fact that they weren't the same people they had been back then, or simply the enchanting location of St Victoria, but it felt so tantalisingly close to the life she had once begun to imagine for her and Liam.

And now they were working together again, just like old times, and little Lucy was at last ready for her procedure. Talia couldn't shake the feeling that it was a portentous day.

Even as she finished gowning Liam, he was speaking with the anaesthetist, confirming the wholly intravenous anaesthesia, and transoesophageal echocardiography that would allow Liam to monitor the heart and valve function without the lungs or ribs getting in the way.

The next time Talia had time to think, the operation was well underway.

A pillow had been positioned under the little girl's right shoulder, a soft tissue retractor helping to open up her chest wall, over the right ventricle, and Talia watched as Liam pulled three deep stay sutures towards him to ensure optimal surgical exposure as she passed him the necessary equipment.

He worked quickly and efficiently, his experience and skill more than evident. And still he talked through what he was doing, allowing her to learn as he went. As if he understood how ner-

vous she was feeling given that that the rest of
the surgical team had experience of this procedure with the previous cardiothoracic surgeon.

There was no doubt that Lucy was in the best
possible hands, and Talia felt a lance of pride as
Liam worked.

So far so good.

'So now I'm placing these pursestring sutures
to avoid any haematoma of the ascending aorta
wall,' he showed her, as she peered over the little girl's body.

'Yes, I see,' Talia confirmed, studying the way
he placed the venous pursestring around the left
atrial appendage—a small ear-shaped sac in the
muscle wall of the left atrium—and reinforced
it using suture pledgets.

If she remembered everything correctly, he
would first place a venous cannula, using the inside of the left ventricle. Then an antegrade flow
cannula would be inserted in the ascending aorta.

But still, watching him work was mesmerising.
It made her feel privileged to be a part of something truly special, and Talia realised that was
something she'd been missing ever since leaving Dukes.

Leaving Liam.

If she had been more a part of Isak's team, it
might have helped. But she suspected that was
only part of it.

'Once we've initiated perfusion, we'll stop the

heart and remove the aortic valve,' he glanced up at her as though reading her thoughts.

This was the part of the operation she didn't know at all. Even though Liam had used this approach back at Duke's she'd never actually been on one of those procedures with him. She tried to remember what she'd read about him suturing the non-stented graft to the left subclavian artery, but as she watched the surgery unfold, it was easier just to watch and absorb than to try to over think it.

Time passed so quickly in the OR, especially watching someone like Liam work, that Talia was almost shocked when Liam concluded his closing.

The operation was over.

And had been successful.

'So how was your first right-anterior thoracotomy?' he asked, almost twenty-four hours later as he was emerging from his hotel suite's shower. 'With a side of frozen-elephant-trunk technique?'

He'd spent most of the past day and night in his office at The Island Clinic, attending to other cases but mostly ensuring that little Lucy Wells didn't suffer any post-surgery complications.

Something she knew he would have loved to have been able to do for every other patient he'd ever operated on.

But a few hours ago, he'd finally allowed him-

self some downtime. He was all hers…and Talia
was definitely enjoying the view. Even the towel,
slung low over his hips, offered her a mouth-watering sight as she reclined, naked and sated, in
his bed.

'Try saying that after a mouthful of those
Dream Fusions.' She laughed, propping herself
up on her elbows. 'The surgery was incredible,
just don't let it go to your head.'

'I'm just relieved there weren't any complications,' he stated evenly. As humble as she remembered him.

'I imagine Nate and Isak feel the same. I take
it you've spoken to them?'

'I briefed Nate, although I know he was hov-
ering about the gallery, watching, a couple of
times.'

'You never let it show.' She drew in a breath,
knowing that her chief's primary concerns would
have been Lucy Wells, and Liam, but hoping that
she had acquitted herself well, all the same.

'Why would I?' He didn't exactly shrug, but
his voice did it for him. 'I'm bringing my A-game
whether my chief is there or not. He isn't going
to change that.'

'That's such a *Liam* thing to say.' She grinned,
dropping a kiss onto his bare, muscled chest
and loving the way he slid his hand instinctively
around the back of her neck as he bowed his head
to kiss her properly.

How was it so easy, so *right* between them? She should have known it couldn't last.

'Nate also mentioned something else,' he began, and she couldn't have said why her stomach flip-flopped. 'Isak has pretty much recovered now, and since Lucy Wells's surgery is now complete...'

'You'll be leaving St Victoria.' Her breath came out in a rush.

'Nate's secretary is looking into flights for me,' he confirmed.

Talia froze, saying nothing though she wanted to ask him why he'd waited until this moment to tell her.

But if he wanted her to go—and something ached deep within her chest at the notion—then he was going to have to say it. She wasn't just going to leave. Not this time. She'd spent three years dreaming of this moment—of being back with Liam—and it was pointless lying about that to herself any longer.

Or lying to him.

'You've fitted in so well that I'm surprised he didn't offer you a permanent role here.' She plastered a bright smile on her face, although she wasn't sure he bought it, especially when he didn't answer, and she could feel the corners of her mouth tugging downwards. 'He did, didn't he?'

'Not in as many words,' Liam hazarded.

She should have taken that as the end of conversation, but something egged her on.

'Which words, then? Precisely?'

For a moment she thought Liam wasn't going to reply. But then he spoke.

'He mentioned that I seemed a good fit and that the team could always use an extra surgeon like me.'

A job offer by any other standards.

'You could always take it,' she heard herself saying. Boldly—if she was being honest. 'You said yourself that any number of surgeons would cut off their own limbs with a scalpel just to get to work here. So what's stopping you? You could easily stay.'

He only hesitated for a beat.

'Why would I do that?'

She wanted to say *her*. But that sounded too arrogant.

'Because I would want you to.' She wrinkled her nose. 'And I thought you might want that as well.'

The silence swirled around them, just like the grey mist that crept in over the jungle part of the island and usually heralded the start of the hurricane season. She could imagine that this storm would be no less brutal.

'I don't.' He spoke at last.

And what did it say about her that she didn't believe him?

'Liam—'

'You don't love me.' He cut her off, his voice abrading her. Almost from the inside out. 'And you don't want me to stay.'

Carefully, she sat up in the bed, pulling the sheet around her, unsure whether to go or to stay. But far from sounding as though he was trying to convince her, it seemed as though he was trying to convince himself.

The thought lent her courage.

'I know what I want, Liam.' She thought she even sounded a touch snippy.

'Really?' he challenged instantly. 'So you want your family to hate you?'

He was warming to the topic now, she could tell by the way he threw the words at her with that hatefully impassive green-eyed stare.

'That's what you're saying you want, is it, Talia?' he pushed her when she didn't answer.

'What? No, of course not, but—'

'Only that's what would happen,' he continued ruthlessly. He was disengaging, she could read it in the set of his jaw and the turn of his body, and she thought it might kill her to see him like this.

'You told me yourself,' he pointed out, and a wiser woman would surely have heeded that tone to his voice. Too controlled and even to be anything other than wholly dangerous.

But she couldn't seem to stop herself.

'No…' she cried. 'Liam, you've got it all wrong.'

'I don't believe I have anything wrong,' he countered quietly.

And whatever emotions she had felt coursing through him these last couple of days had clearly been stuffed firmly back down. Now he was pulling on that armour of detachment that he always wore.

And Talia hated it. *Hated it.* Even though, more and more, she was beginning to think it had never suited him at all.

'That night after going to Auntie Zinia's, you avoided the parade and you told me that you didn't want your brothers to see you with me. You said that they had only just forgiven you for being with me three years when you should have been home with your family. With your mother.'

'But—'

'You said that to me, did you not?'

'Yes, but…' she faltered, flustered. 'They're still teenagers, they haven't met someone they love yet. They don't understand.'

'What about your father, Talia? Is he a teenager?'

'Of course not.'

'But I'm guessing he blames me, too.'

She didn't answer. What could she say?'

'And if he feels that way about me,' Liam forged on, 'how would he feel if you left St Victoria again? With me?'

'They would come round,' she said hesitantly.

The worst of it was that she wasn't even sure they would.

'I won't accept that,' Liam ground out. 'I won't have you lose them. You don't know what it's like not to have anyone, Talia. But I do. And I wouldn't wish that on anyone.'

'We would have each other,' she ventured.

'No. I can't be that someone for you, Talia. I don't know how to love. And I certainly can't take the place of your father, your brothers or your beloved grandmother. Even all the people you know here on this island. People who love you. People like Nyla.'

'You could try,' she whispered.

'I wouldn't want to,' he told her flatly, his cloak of indifference now firmly back in place.

She wanted to reach and tear it off him, or at the very least press her palm against his cheek and make him see all the good in himself that she saw. She could wrap her arms around him and pour herself into all the ways she loved him— had once loved him. But she didn't dare. It might lead to physical proximity but it wouldn't close that emotional divide between them. Not even an inch.

And she thought that was what destroyed her most of all.

Liam hated himself.

Talia's pain was so utterly evident. And knowing he had been the one to cause it made that black thing inside him—the one that might have been a heart in anyone else—splinter and cleave, but he told himself he couldn't weaken. For Talia's sake.

He couldn't bear to see her give up everything she cared for, everyone she loved, for him. A man who was so damaged and irreparable that he couldn't possibly be good for her.

Yet there was something about her willingness and her ferocity that lodged in his chest. Right *there*. A tiny ball so hot and bright as the magnificent St Victorian sun that he thought it might, for the rest of his life, light his way and keep him warm in those cold, lonely moments when he returned to North Carolina.

There would never be anyone else for him but Talia—he now knew that for a fact. But she deserved better than him. More than he could ever offer. More than this man who had just broken her.

But he should have known that his feisty, strong, powerful Talia wouldn't be stay that way for long. He watched transfixed as she appeared to straighten her back and elongate her limbs, still filling his bed in the most tempting way.

She craned her neck to look up at him. Her voice was quiet but true.

'Will you answer me something?'

He ought to refuse.

'Anything,' he bit out instead.

Foolishly.

She flicked her tongue out over her lips, and even though he knew there was nothing sexual in it, it did nothing to stop that spiral of desire from curving its way down his spine.

'What happened between you and your father?'

Desperation might as well have been a hand reaching into her chest and squeezing. This was not a conversation he cared to have. It wasn't one he ever *had* had with anyone. Ever.

Yet he was filled with a surprising need to accommodate her in any way he could.

'My mother died in childbirth.' Liam stilled as the atmosphere in the room seemed to change in an instant.

It went from urgent and cold to raw and jagged in what felt like a heartbeat. A shimmering menace skirting around the edges of the clean walls and tasteful décor. But Talia didn't seem to have noticed, which meant it was all in his head.

'I'm so sorry.' She was shaking her head, obviously getting over the shock of his announcement faster than he was. 'I know you told me she died when you were younger, but I didn't realise.'

'How could you have?' he clipped out. 'I've not mentioned it before.'

'It must have been so hard for you, growing up without her.'

'Harder for my father. She was the love of my father's life. He has never cared for anyone the way he cared for her.'

'Except for you.' She nodded, thinking she understood.

And he could have left it at that, with Talia thinking he'd opened up and that she knew more now. He didn't *have* to say anything more.

'No, he's never cared for anyone else, especially not me.'

Confusion lapped in her eyes like the soft waves on the shore behind them. For a brief moment he wondered what it must be like to have a family care so much for you that you couldn't quite grasp the idea of a father not loving his child. Then he shut it down because, frankly, what was the point of even thinking that way?

'Especially not you?' she prompted gently, when he didn't say anything else.

He told himself to stop talking, but the words kept coming.

'My father has never forgiven me.'

'Forgiven you?' Her brow knitted in confusion. 'I don't understand.'

He waited, suppressing the urge to ball his hands into fists to fight off the gamut of...*feelings* that were crowding around the periphery of his mind.

Her face cleared abruptly, then assumed an expression of abhorrence.

'He *blamed* you?'

'She died in childbirth, and I was the baby.' It took all Liam had to keep his tone even. 'As far as my father was concerned, the cause and effect were undeniable.'

Was he really trying to explain his complicated relationship with the old man to Talia? He had never felt the need to explain himself to anyone, ever. More than that, he could never have allowed himself to be so vulnerable in front of anyone before—even Talia. Yet now there was something inside him making him say things he told himself he didn't want to say.

'That's nonsense,' she snorted delicately.

'My father feels otherwise.'

'He really blamed you?' Talia asked tentatively, her voice shaking as if she couldn't quite believe it.

'He was grieving.' Liam shrugged. Because what else was there to say?

Talia, it seemed, was having none of it. Her expression was growing tighter and angrier by the minute. *For* him. Another ball of warmth and light to file away for later.

'And you're making excuses for him? What about your grief?'

'I didn't know her.' The words came naturally. An echo of a thousand times his father had ever spoken to him, and he'd grown to believe it in time. More than that, he'd evolved to feel that way. 'You can't lose what you never had to begin with.'

'You can't really believe that!' Talia exclaimed. 'She was your *mother*, and you never even got the opportunity to meet her. Of course you can grieve. How can you think you don't have that right?'

'Because I don't,' he answered simply.

Because his father had told him, over and over, from the moment he was born. And because, no matter what logic as an adult might dictate, the bald statement was so deep inside him—so ingrained—that Liam had never felt any different.

He didn't know how to.

'So why are you telling me any of this?' she asked softly, with a tinge of sadness that shot right to his core.

'I want you to understand.'

'Understand what, exactly?' Again, that gentle voice that threatened to creep under his skin.

He fought against it.

'That this is who I am. This is why I can't be the man you want me to be. I was never him.'

'I don't believe that,' she disagreed, shaking her curls furiously. 'You're more than just an extension of someone else, here to make amends for an event that happened at your birth, and over which you had absolutely no control. You deserve more than that, Liam. You always have.'

And Liam couldn't say what it was about her reaction that made him feel less...broken. As though he wasn't as culpable as he'd somehow believed.

'He blamed me for a reason, Talia.'

'No, he took his grief out on you,' she countered. 'A baby. And it was the cruellest, saddest thing he could have done. But that doesn't make you all those horrible things he's always told you that you are. And you're not the only one with regrets, Liam.'

'The only regret you should have is ever meeting me,' he told her vehemently.

'I don't believe that. And if you really believe it then it's a problem we're going to have to work on. Together.'

She sounded so positive, so hopeful it scraped at him. He braced himself against the unwelcome sentiment. That wasn't the point of this conversation.

*What was the point of it, then?* a snide voice echoed in his mind, but he shoved it aside.

Talia needed to believe there was more to him than there was. She wanted to understand why he didn't love her the way he suspected she had once loved him. She didn't understand why he wasn't capable of doing so, and he'd never been able to tell her.

But perhaps now he could.

Maybe this was his chance to finally show himself to her for who he really was. Prove to her, once and for all, that he wasn't worth her attention or kindness. This could be his final gift to her before he left the island.

'No, you're not listening to me,' he bit out. 'There is no *we*.'

His voice was harsher than he'd intended but that couldn't be helped. He felt more broken now, opening up to Talia, than he ever had before.

And yet, somehow, something inside him felt more...*whole* than it had in a long time. Perhaps ever.

'Was there no one else?' Her voice cut across his thoughts, shocking him.

There was no hurt in her tone, it was simply brimming with compassion. He hated that he didn't deserve it.

'Tell me more about your grandmother.'

'I told you, I don't remember much.' He tried to dismiss the question but that felt too much like dismissing Talia, and suddenly he found he couldn't bring himself to do that.

'I have a few vague memories of her. She made life more...bearable. I think I remember her arguing with my father, and then she was never around again. Whether she'd cared for me or not, the long and short of it was that it wasn't enough to stick around. *I* wasn't enough to stick around for.'

'You don't know that, Liam.' Talia shook her head vehemently. 'You've never told me about your father before, but he seems…awful. I'm sorry, but it's true. Maybe your grandmother had no choice.'

'Maybe,' was all he replied.

Because he'd told himself that same thing for years to make himself feel better. But when it came down to it, it didn't matter if it was true or a lie, it still meant she'd walked away and he'd been left alone with a man who resented his very existence.

'And there was no one else at all?' she hedged, after a few moments.

'I don't need anyone else.'

It occurred to him that his choice of tense was all too telling.

'We all need someone, Liam. Someone to fight for us. To be on our side.'

'You aren't listening to me,' he growled, but far from backing off she looked all the more caring.

'On the contrary, I've heard everything you said.'

He glowered at her for a long, long moment, but she didn't budge. She didn't even blink. It finally became clear to him that she wasn't going to relent. And, to his shock, he found himself capitulating instead.

'There's been no one.' His tone tried to show her how little that mattered to him.

'Then that's truly sad,' she told him simply, her eyes conveying so much more than he thought he could bear. 'I can't imagine how difficult that must be. I always had my parents, and if I hadn't had them then I could at least go to my gramma.'

'So now do you understand why I can't allow you to lose all of that for me? A man who they hate?'

'They would come to accept it once they saw that I was happy,' she argued fiercely. 'I would make them.'

And it didn't help that what she wanted was the same thing he wanted too. Deep down—where he'd tried to bury it. But even if he couldn't give her that, he could give her something better. He could give Talia her freedom.

'But I'm not the one to make you happy, Talia,' he ground out. 'So even if you brought them round, it would change nothing. Nothing at all.'

It felt like an eternity passed as they remained face to face, with her on the bed and him in his towel. And his stone-of-a-heart was more leaden than he'd ever known it.

His case load was clear, and his main-case, little Lucy Wells would soon be able to be discharged. It had yet to be decided whether he

would fly to Los Angeles—where Lucy and Violet lived—or whether Isak would take over the
post-op follow-ups now that the man was back,
but either way Liam would be leaving St Victoria
in a few days. And he wouldn't return.

He would be alone. Just like always.

Just as he preferred.

# CHAPTER THIRTEEN

TALIA FELT AS though she was in mourning.

Liam had said that he couldn't lose what he'd never had to begin with, but she didn't agree. She'd never had Liam, not really; and yet that was exactly how she felt—as though she was losing him.

It was as though the freer, less-constrained Liam she'd been getting to know over the course of the past couple of weeks was at war with the man loaded down with assumed responsibilities and unrealistic expectations she'd known back in North Carolina.

Only now she understood him better. This clever, funny but detached man who had evidently been told how little he was worth his entire life, right from the cradle. Hated by the very person who should have loved his infant son the most, the person who should have protected his baby boy the most fiercely. But he hadn't. He'd blame an innocent baby for a tragedy that Liam could have no more understood back then than prevented.

But all that had turned Liam into the driven, focussed man he was now. So what was she supposed to do about it? She couldn't change who he was or what he believed, and she'd already tried being there for him and showing that she loved him.

Hadn't she?

'You accused me of leaving three years ago without even a note, and I never explained myself. The truth is that I didn't leave because of something you said, or did, I left because of what you *couldn't* say.'

'And you were right to,' Liam said. It was more of a statement than a question, and without a hint of censure in his tone. As though there was nothing left to say.

Talia couldn't breathe. Desperation wound through her, lending sudden urgency. It felt like she'd only just found Liam after all these years. He'd finally let her in yet now she was about to lose this last precious opportunity.

'You aren't the only one with scars, Liam,' she choked out.

It was like a band tightening around her; the truth, squatting on her chest with a weight that she didn't think she could stand any longer. She wanted to tell him. To show him her own wounds. She pushed gently back from him and when she spoke, her voice was little more than a whisper.

'I knew.'

Liam didn't answer. In some ways she was grateful for that.

'I knew something was wrong long before that final call from my father.'

It was almost unbearable—hanging in the air, almost acrid. At least to her.

Liam waited.

'All the signs had been there for months...if only I'd chosen to read them. The way her face had been getting more and more pinched. The heaviness around her eyes.'

'There could have been any number of explanations for that.' He knew where she was heading and he wished he could spare her the guilt. 'You can't torture yourself like that.'

'I didn't even take the time to ask her, though. I didn't even spot it.'

'Because of me,' he stated flatly, hearing the accusation that was there, even if she hadn't voiced it. 'I've ended up causing pain to anyone who might dare to care for me, Talia. Can't you see that?'

Yet more proof of how he brought darkness and anguish to those around him. His mother, his accursed father, and now even his extraordinary Talia.

'That's nonsense,' she refuted. 'I didn't spot it by my own choice. Because I didn't want to see it, I guess. Maybe because that would have meant I'd have to do something about it, and I was too selfish to return home.'

'You weren't selfish,' he countered immediately. 'You just didn't notice it because you trusted your family to tell you something like that, but they kept it from you. And before you get defensive, I'm not criticising them, they only kept it from you because they didn't want you to worry. They wanted you to enjoy the new life you'd found for yourself in North Carolina.'

'Is it any wonder, after I'd complained at them so many times that I wanted more for my life than growing up on a small island?'

'You can't beat yourself up for that, Talia, it was perfectly natural for you to have wanted to spread your wings.'

She didn't point out that Liam hadn't spread his wings, that he'd allowed himself to be fettered by the guilt of causing his mother's death. She couldn't have even if she'd wanted to, she was too caught up in her own grief.

'I made them feel like they weren't enough. Like she wasn't enough,' Talia choked.

'I would say that you made her feel like she'd raised a bold, confident woman who wanted to see more of the world. But in the end you realised that home was the place you wanted to be. Wasn't that precisely what you said when you talked about setting something you love free?'

She didn't answer, she simply drew her knees up to her chest and dropped her chin on them.

'So why didn't you simply tell me this, Talia?'

'I don't know,' she lied.

'I think you do.'

And despite all her cautions to herself, Talia could feel things beginning to shift inside her. He'd revealed so much to her tonight. Well, perhaps not *so* much but definitely more than she had ever imagined he would. She couldn't help but wonder if she'd finally found a way to bypass that ancient armour of his.

So how could she expect him to trust her more if she couldn't equally trust him?

'I didn't tell you because… Oh, there wasn't just one reason.' She shook her head uncertainly. 'I don't know if I thought I'd be back or not. I think a part of me thought I would. I had no idea how bad it was with Mama so I could never have imagined that she would…that I would lose her.'

'I was sorry to hear that, you know,' he told her quietly, and the gently sincerity in his voice was unmistakable.

'You've said that once already.' She jerked her head in a semblance of a nod but she didn't add that knowing he could never confide in her, open up to her had been the proverbial final straw.

That every day that he'd kept himself from her had hurt that little more and, despite it all, nothing less than her mama's illness could have torn

her away from him. Even though she'd known it
wasn't the healthiest relationship, she'd been too
addicted to him.

Was still addicted, if she was honest. Because
it felt as though his admission about his father
had been opening the door a crack, and she was
already there, metaphorically trying to jam her
foot in the minuscule gap before he could slam
it shut again.

She couldn't accept that in a matter of days he
would be leaving St Victoria. It seemed too cruel.

As if on cue, the bedside phone rang and Talia
didn't need him to answer to know what it was
about. It seemed even fate was conspiring against
them.

She remained immobile, wrapped in her sheet
on his bed as Liam crossed the room, the white
towel still clinging lovingly to his form.

The parallels weren't ideal.

As he answered the call, she listened to his
monosyllabic words of acknowledgement. His
gruff thanks and the click as he replaced the re-
ceiver.

'Arrangements for your flight?' she asked at
last into the silence.

'Yes,' Liam answered.

And then, when she couldn't bear the stillness
any longer, 'When?'

'Tomorrow morning.'

A whoosh of breath escaped her.

'So soon,' she managed.

He didn't reply. But, then, she supposed, what was there to say? And that truth twisted inside her even as she could feel the inferno building from the pit of her belly, hot and needy, and enough to burn her from the inside out. He was leaving and all she could think was that she wanted him one last time. And that a perverse part of her almost welcomed the pain of closure.

So why not put it all on the line?

He needed to move. At the very least, he needed to step back away from the bed, away from the temptation of Talia.

He did neither. He simply stayed where he was, and he had no idea how long he stared at her, watching a host of emotions chase through her lovely, expressive eyes. He was only aware of the furore raging inside him. Devouring him from the inside, then threatening to burst out of him at any moment, wild and unrestrained.

He still hadn't fully processed the fact that he'd talked to her about his father. Telling her things he had never dreamed he would tell anyone. It ought to have alarmed him enough to send him out that hotel door instantly.

Had he forgotten how Talia had left him three

years ago? Or how long it had taken to piece himself back together?

Another person abandoning him. Discarding him.

Breaking all his rules could only be deleterious; it only proved that he really was as damaged as he'd ever feared. Worse—as much as his father had always told him.

But the worst of it was that even through everything he said to her, and the fact that he was trying to push her away, the only thing he really wanted to do was to pull her closer than ever.

He wasn't aware of moving or approaching the bed, but suddenly there he was. He reached out and moved a stray curl off her damp cheek.

But, Lord, he wanted to do so much more.

Haltingly, she pulled her head back, her lips parted and her breathing shallow, betraying the fact that she felt the same way.

'We agreed no more.' His voice cracked.

'*You* said no more.' She eyed him steadfastly. 'I didn't. I asked you to stay. So it's up to you, Liam. I'm not the one waging some kind of internal war.'

'You just told me how you regret what happened with your mother. You lost sight of yourself because of me.'

'I regret that I didn't pay more attention,' she concurred. 'And that I was self-absorbed. But I didn't lose sight of myself because of you. And, even if I had, I know who I am now. Just as I know what I want. Even so, if you want to finish this once and for all, I'll go now.'

And even though he knew he should, he found he couldn't. He didn't have the mental strength to do it again, not knowing that in twenty-four hours he would be gone. That he would never see her again. Or touch her. Or taste her.

He'd pushed her away too many times. This time was different. And as he reached for her, admiring her grace as she knelt up on the bed before he hauled her back into his arms, Liam thought that she'd never looked so soft or at peace.

She was right, she was no longer that girl he'd known in North Carolina—and he was no longer that man.

But he still wasn't enough for her. *That hasn't changed*, Liam reminded himself.

But he wasn't listening.

He wanted her too much. *His Talia*—a woman who knew her own mind. He found that more tempting than anything and he couldn't resist her. More to the point, he didn't want to.

'I can't offer you more than this,' he muttered.

'I know.' Talia ran her hand down his chest slowly and deliberately. 'Maybe in a different life. Or a different time.'

Or if he had been a different man. But he didn't voice that one.

'You're sure?' he ground out.

'That I want you?' She sounded breathless and incredulous all at once. 'Liam, I'm sure.'

Liam couldn't hold back a low growl. It was a pale echo of the howling that he felt inside but audible all the same. He sank back down on the bed, discarding his towel and her bedsheet in one efficient movement.

And then he flipped on his back, lifted his Talia into the air and settled her on top of him.

She looked magnificent. More vibrant and full of life than he'd ever seen her before, and he stilled, drinking her in. If this was one of the last images he was ever going to have with her then he wanted to remember it in every last, stunning detail.

Something shifted inside him. A jolt and a start, as if his long-dead heart had just kicked back into life. But he pretended he didn't care about that. He wasn't going to overthink it any more. She was offering him tonight and he would move heaven and earth to take her up on it. Even if it was all he could give her.

By this time tomorrow he would be gone. He could deal with the fallout then.

If she was going to give herself to him one more time, Talia told herself ferociously as Liam settled her over him and stared at her as though she was the most precious thing in the world, she was going to make it count.

Really count.

She basked in the way he gazed at her—as if she was infinitely precious to him—and then revelled in the way he let his hands wander over her, smoothing his way and setting every inch of her skin alight in the process. She decided he knew just how badly he was driving her crazy when he trailed his tongue over her bare flesh and straight past her aching, straining nipples.

He skimmed his fingers down the sides of her torso, snaking over her belly and splaying his hands across her skin as he tested her and teased her. But none of that was anything compared to the way he gazed at her.

Three years ago, she'd loved the way he'd studied her, his eyes so green as they'd glittered with undisguised hunger. Even greed. He'd always made her feel so very beautiful and desired. But now…?

Now there was a different edge to his gaze. Desire, yes; but also something else. Something deeper. Something that made her feel not just wanted but needed. Adored. He made her feel precious.

He made her think she could see a future.

*This is just about living in the moment*, she thought in a panic, shaking such dangerous notions from her head and forcing herself back to the present. And it was almost a blessing when he lowered his head to take one nipple, lace bra included, into his mouth, as all other distractions fell away.

He lavished attention on one breast, his hand cupping her gently while his tongue drew whorls and patterns over her nipple. Abrading her skin and heightening her sensitivity. Once he was satisfied with one side, Liam shifted to the other, until she was shivering with pleasure, her breathing harsh and fast as she begged him for more.

Instead, he walked his hand down her body, over the swell of her stomach and beyond until he was circling around her sex, making it thrum with longing. Instinctively, Talia raised her hips, wanting more contact, more friction.

'Patience,' he murmured, still tracing his lazy shapes around her but never touching where she needed him most. 'All in good time.'

She groaned, resisting the urge to roll her hips again, knowing he would only punish her by prolonging the wait. That deliciously wicked streak that she'd always loved. Reaching her hands out, she slid them through his hair instead, as if that might somehow ground her when he finally ended this exquisite torture.

'Better,' he muttered, letting his knuckles graze over her.

If he continued like this then she feared she was going to come apart with him barely even touching her.

And then, finally, he twisted his wrist around

and cupped her, her molten heat spilling out over his palm.

'So beautiful.' Dipping his head, he kissed her again. 'So perfect.'

Then before she could move, or even register what he was doing, he was sliding his fingers into her slick centre. Talia groaned, rolling her hips again and needing more contact as he played with her, almost sending her mindless with need.

She could feel that fire building already, racing her to the edge far faster than she was prepared for, but she couldn't do anything about it. Liam was all she'd dreamed of this past week, replaying their weekend together over and over again, thinking that was all she would ever have. And now they were back here, and she didn't think she could hold on much longer.

It was too fast. Too…rushed.

'Relax,' Liam murmured, dropping a final kiss on her abdomen before choosing the moment to flip them both around. He moved to the end of the bed while she pushed herself up onto her elbows to watch, a savage hunger joining that fire inside.

He was magnificent. He was always magnificent. His athletic physique a symphony of rock-solid ridges and corded muscles. And this time, when he lowered himself onto the bed on top of her, Talia gripped his shoulders and turned him over as she moved astride him.

'That's how you want to play it?' he rasped. A rich, throaty sound.

'That's exactly how I want to play it.' She moved her hands reverently over that incredible body, committing every last millimetre of him to memory, though she couldn't have said why.

She tasted him and teased him, grazed his skin gently with her teeth then followed with her tongue. Her hands, her mouth slid over that hewn chest, the rippling stomach muscles and that perfect V-shape where his lower abs moved against his obliques like tectonic plates shifting beneath the earth's crust to create the Bec Range that they had admired together a lifetime ago.

And he was every bit as awe-inspiring.

It was only as she moved lower that Liam caught her hips and moved her back up his body, and she couldn't help but think that she'd always loved how his hands were so large and powerful that it always made her feel all the more feminine and dainty.

Then he shifted position so that her heat was pressed against the hardest part of him, and she didn't think any more. She just felt. Letting him lift her slightly as his blunt tip edged into her, taking it slowly as she braced against his shoulders, her breath catching in her throat.

It took Talia a moment to realise that he was letting her control the pace. Letting her rock against him, her body thrumming and clamouring for him, as it always had. Leaning forward, she laid her body over his, every inch of them touching as she let him cup her cheeks with his palms and trace her jaw with his fingers.

Then, very languidly, very deliberately she reached down between them and took hold of him, wrapping her fingers around his long, thick length and testing his heavy, glorious weight in her hand. He groaned, and she exulted in the sheer freeness of the sound. Wishing it was a sound she could hear for ever.

There was something about being here, on St Victoria, that made her feel unburdened and lighter, in a way that she'd never felt back in North Carolina.

Or perhaps it was she who was different. Or Liam.

A stab of sadness shot through her, swiftly followed by a shot of urgency. He couldn't stay here any more than she could return to Duke's. So if this was all they were going to have, she wasn't about waste it on melancholy and *what–ifs*. Guiding him back to her softness, she began to move again, rocking against him as she moved back up to a seated position and then taking him inside her heat.

'So tight.' Liam groaned again, and a tremble rolled through her.

She inched down again to the same response, and again, until he was as deep as he could be.

Then she lifted off him and did it all again in a private tango all their own. A bliss like no other as they built up the rhythm, lazy and indulgent at first, picking up pace and urgency in time, that edge heading towards her, faster and faster.

And then, suddenly, he reached down between them to press down where she ached most, and she felt herself catapulting over that abyss. Tumbling and falling with no safety net as he surged inside her, and as they plummeted back to earth together she couldn't help calling out his name.

Or the fact that she loved him.

But she didn't realise that she'd actually voiced it aloud until he froze against her, his length still inside her but no longer holding her as he had been a moment ago. The bliss around them shattered, with no way to piece it back together.

Well, she'd told herself to put it all the line for him, and this was undoubtedly a spectacular way of doing precisely that.

# CHAPTER FOURTEEN

THE DECLARATION HUNG in the air between them and, for what felt like an eternity Liam was too stunned to answer. And then, suddenly, he lifted her off him and flipped from the bed, grabbing a pair of cargo shorts in the process and hauling them on.

How could such beautiful, simple words actually sound so damned ugly? Or perhaps it was more that they made him *feel* ugly, because they reminded him of the truth he'd spent the past weeks pretending didn't exist.

Or maybe it was because a wretched part of him bellowed to echo it back to her—and that was a terrifying thought because he was already fighting the urge to acquiesce to her early suggestion of staying on St Victoria.

'No, you don't,' he bit out eventually, stalking the room.

His voice was too controlled and yet razor-sharp, as if he could silence her. As if he could reverse the last thirty seconds by sheer force of will alone.

Because even if he did say it back, and even if he thought he might mean it—somehow—he knew it would be duplicitous since he didn't understand the concept of love. Not really. However much he wanted to.

And that meant, in the end, he would end up letting her down. Hurting her.

'I love you,' she repeated, quiet but firm, wrapping herself up in the pure white bedsheet that somehow only served to enhance her appearance of fragility. And made him feel even worse, as impossible as that was.

'You're wrong.' He gritted his teeth. 'Mistaken. Whatever you're feeling right now, it isn't...*that*.'

He'd silenced the rage inside him for all these years—because *love* wasn't something that had ever been crafted for him. Yet right here, right now, the rage was nothing compared to that part of him that ached to be able to say those three simple words back to her. That wished he wasn't so damaged.

It didn't help that Talia somehow looked both stunned and defiant at her unexpected confession.

'First you tell me that I don't know what I mean when I ask you to stay,' she retorted, an echo of their earlier conversation. But, just like then, he heard the tremor in her voice. 'Now you're saying I know what I feel.'

'That's exactly what I'm saying.'

'Well, I dare say I know better than you do,

given that these are *my* emotions. And given that you can't even bring yourself to utter the word.'

'Emotions aren't real. And at best, *love*...' He paused for a fraction of a second, that one word—four simple letters—taking an age to fall off his tongue. Then he regrouped. 'It's like temporary inebriation after the brain has had a cocktail shot of norepinephrine, dopamine, phenylethylamine.'

He stopped, terribly afraid it wasn't the sound of the word he hated as much as his inability to really understand all it stood for. If their earlier conversation had thrown him, he didn't want to think how this one might go.

Which was all the more reason to end it. Now. He told Talia as much.

'Liam, do you know what you sound like?' she asked gently, almost pityingly.

And he thought that was what he hated most of all. That, and the growing suspicion that she might be right.

Yet he forged on anyway.

'At worst, it's a weapon that the cruellest of humans use to wield against the people they claim to care for the most.'

Too late, he realised he was giving away too much. Exposing his own vulnerabilities by revealing how his father, his grandmother, even Talia herself had managed to hurt him.

'I'm sorry.' She shook her head, leaving him in no doubt that she was sorrier for *him* than actually sorry for what she'd said. 'I know you don't believe in it, and believe me that I never meant to say it.'

'So you're taking it back?' he demanded.

It struck him suddenly that he didn't even know whether he wanted her to take it back or not. But, worse, he knew he would accept it if she did. Take it at face value, and continue where they'd left off barely a few minutes before.

The way he had after their last conversation. So what did it mean that he would readily pretend she'd never uttered the words?

Instead, Talia seemed to sit up straighter on the bed, proud and strong. And looking almost ethereal.

'I don't take it back, Liam.' She shrugged her shoulders. 'I didn't mean to say it, granted, but it's true all the same. I love you. That's why I suggested you stay on St Victoria before. Why I still want you to stay now.'

Something sat on his chest, squashing the air out of him. He fought to surface.

'I don't accept that.'

'Because you fear it.' She held her hands up as if to soothe him.

As if he was some wounded wild animal who couldn't understand anything else. The worst of it was that was partly how he felt.

'I don't fear it,' he denied angrily. 'I just don't *believe* in it.'

'After everything your father put you through as a child, that's understandable. As is your desire never to have children, for fear of putting them through the same. But can't you see that will never happen?'

He heard the plea in her voice and, for a moment, he almost went to her. Because the truth of it was that he wanted nothing more than to believe her. But he'd had this dream before, three years ago, when she had told him the same thing. A few days later she'd left him.

He'd thought he'd been setting her free by letting her leave and not chasing her down and now, despite everything that had happened between them this past month, he knew that if he still wanted her to be free, this time he was going to have to be the one to walk away.

Because he only ever wrecked things.

'You're letting your dreadful father win again, can't you see that?' Talia begged softly.

'I told you that,' he faltered, not wanting to examine why he *had* told her that, 'by way of explanation. Not as ammunition for you to now use against me.'

'You would think that opening up to a person automatically means they're using it as ammunition.'

He blew out scornfully, but she forged on.

'I don't know what your father did to make your grandmother leave, but I have to believe that she left to protect you somehow. It's clear that she loved you a great deal because even through your fuzzy memories I see the kind, patient man you are today and I know that had to have come from someone. From her.'

'You see what you want to see, Talia.'

'And if I did, is that such a great flaw? That I should want to see that goodness and kindness and love in you?'

'It isn't love,' he gritted out, but it was becoming harder and harder to sound convincing.

And the more he tried to distance himself, the more she seemed to level observations at him that he wished, oh, so fervently were true. If only he was a man as promising as the one she was describing.

If only he was worthy of her. But he wasn't.

And maybe she was right about him letting his old man win, but what choice was there? Even if everything he'd been learning about himself this past week were true, even if he was finally beginning to have his eyes opened, it didn't change the man he'd been for most of his life.

Maybe he hadn't set out as the bleak, corrupted kid that his father had told him he was, but he'd certainly become that person over the years. Not least when first his grandmother and then Talia had proved that to be true.

Pain rained down on him, like tiny shards of ice. He grasped at them as if they were somehow going to save him, even though a part of him recognised, on some level, that it was only because it was easier to be angry than it was to face his greatest fears.

He'd opened up to her in their last conversation, and look where that had got him. He sure as hell wasn't about to make that mistake again.

Instead, he focussed on telling himself that it was almost incomprehensible that *this* woman, of all people, would dare to talk of love to him.

Talia had waited, her breath caught in her throat, unable to inhale or exhale. Silently, she'd willed him to trust her. To come back to her. And for one long, heart-stopping moment she'd thought he was going to.

But then he took another step back and folded his arms across his chest, distancing himself— the way he had always done in the past—his cargo shorts riding so low on his hips that she could see that perfect V where his obliques met his abdomen.

And it struck her that it somehow seemed so intimate a view in the face of such a hostile conversation. As though his mind might be trying to shut her out but his body certainly wasn't.

That begged the question—was he more furious at her for telling him she loved him or himself for wanting to believe it?

Maybe she was reading too much into things

and giving herself false hope, but she was inclined to believe it was the latter.

'I love you and I think you love me too.'

'You've got the wrong man, Talia. That isn't me.'

His face hardened and something cracked in her chest and broke.

'I wish you could see yourself as others do,' she murmured sadly. 'As I do. And look at the stories you've started to tell me about your grandmother. They aren't the memories of a kid who never believed in love, which is all the more reason for you to realise how powerful that emotion can be. How the love of just that one person carried you through those years in spite of everything else.'

'I told you that in confidence,' he bit back. 'Not for you to analyse me. Certainly not for you to use it against me.'

'I wasn't—'

'You were,' he cut in harshly. 'You thought you could level a few so-called *home truths* at me and I'd fall at your feet in gratitude. I can tell you that isn't going to happen, Talia. But allow me to do the same for you.'

And she didn't like that clipped voice or those cold eyes. Not one bit.

'Liam—'

'You talk of my father and my grandmother.

You speak of love, and how it's a powerful emotion. Shall I tell you what I know of *love*?' He practically spat the word out, as if the very taste of it was toxic in his mouth. 'I know that people use it to excuse their behaviour. My father used his *love* of my mother to excuse the way he treated me.'

'You father doesn't know what love is.'

'My grandmother told me she loved me,' he continued, as though Talia hadn't even spoken. 'She promised that she'd always be there to protect me from my father, and then she simply abandoned me to him. And then there's you.'

'No… Liam…'

Talia knew exactly where she was going before he said any more. Her heart punched into her chest, almost winding her. But there was nothing she could do to stop it.

'You were the one who spoke of *love*,' he said harshly. 'But love is about more than words. It's about actions. And you proved to me, beyond all question, three years ago that you don't know anything more about love than I do.'

A kind of desolation began to fill her. She wanted to argue but found she couldn't.

'You claim to love me, Talia, but you were the one who walked out back then without even a word.'

Just like his grandmother had, she realised.

Liam didn't actually say the words but they hung there in the air, strangling and weighty, all the same.

'You know that was because I'd just had the call from my mother.'

'I understand why you had to leave,' he countered grimly. 'I'm pointing out that the way you left isn't *love*. You could have told me. You should have.'

'Yes, well, hindsight is twenty-twenty, isn't it?' There was a bitter hint to her own tone that she hadn't been expecting.

'Tell me one thing, Talia. If the circumstances were the same, would you change things or would you make the same decision over again?'

She wanted to answer. She wanted to tell him there was so much that she would change if she could. But as much as the thoughts swirled and crammed in her head, nothing came out of her mouth.

How could she change any of it? Maybe if her mother hadn't been ill, and she hadn't had to return home. Perhaps if her father hadn't fallen into depression and her brothers hadn't needed her help. Or conceivably if Liam had been able to tell her once, just *once,* that he loved her.

But a do-over changed none of those factors. So how could she choose any other path but the one she had chosen before?

'Just as I thought,' he answered for her, when

it was clear she couldn't—wouldn't—answer for herself. And she thought it was that wholly dispassionate tone that hurt the most. 'Which is why you aren't what I want.'

Misery swelled inside her but she forced it back. His words were intended to cause maximum effect, hurting her the way she'd hurt him three years ago. He wanted to push her away and a few weeks ago, when he'd first arrived on the island, it might have worked. She might have believed him.

But they'd spent so much time together since then that the words no longer fitted. He cared for her more than he wanted to admit to her. Possibly more than he wanted to admit to himself.

'Do you even know what you do want, though?' she asked gently.

He offered a scornful laugh, but it sounded too hollow for her to believe.

'I'm a surgeon, Talia, I save lives every day. How could I want anything more than that?'

Her heart might well have broken at the loneliness of that image. He was the most intelligent, skilled, handsome man she'd ever known. The most incredible surgeon she'd ever watched perform any operation.

But somewhere deep inside him there were still traces of that broken kid he'd once been, and he thought it was too late to fix that. He thought he was too damaged. And she was partly to blame for that.

She owed to him—and to herself—to fight for him this time.

'You're also a man, Liam. A human being.' She was almost pleading with him. 'We aren't designed to be completely alone. There's a reason they say that everybody needs someone.'

'And there are always exceptions to every rule.'

'Even if that's true, you aren't that exception. You think you're too damaged to ever love or be loved. But that isn't true.'

'Believe me when I tell you that you are wrong.' And it was the bleakness in his gaze that cut her deepest. 'I am more damaged that you can ever imagine.'

'You're not,' she whispered. 'You're good, and kind, and self-sacrificing.'

For a moment she thought he was wavering. Taking a moment to let her words sink in. And maybe that was true—for that moment. But then his jaw pulled so tight that she could see a tic flicking irritably. As though he was angry at himself for even entertaining what she was saying.

'This isn't making your case for you, Talia,' he ground out. 'Allow me to prove it. I don't want you. I want a woman I can trust. Whose word I can believe. I don't want someone who says one thing but then acts a different way.'

'Where is this coming from?' she gasped.

But she was afraid she already knew.

He'd opened up to her—finally—when he'd told her about his father. The first time he'd ever really talked in any significant detail about his past. And then he'd received the confirmation of his flight and now he was regretting his moment of perceived weakness.

It wouldn't matter how much she told him that confiding in her was the ultimate strength, he wouldn't believe her.

He didn't trust her. That much was true.

'I'm leaving tomorrow, Talia, to go back to North Carolina. And Duke's.'

Not *home*, she noted joylessly, his words scraping her raw inside. That meant that St Victoria could be his home as well as anywhere else. She opened her mouth to speak but let it close again, resignation pouring through her.

Liam had said that love was about actions, not words. So there was nothing she could say that would ever change his mind about her.

For the first time she felt defeated.

'I should go,' she murmured, silently praying for him to ask her to stay.

His expression remained as closed off as ever.

'I think that would be best.'

Talia jerked her head in a semblance of acknowledgement. She'd lost him, it was impossible to pretend otherwise.

Whatever these last few weeks had been about,

it hadn't been about picking up where they'd left off. They'd already agreed that at the beginning of his brief trip out here to St Victoria.

The simple fact remained: she'd lost him three years ago.

# CHAPTER FIFTEEN

'I ASKED NOT to be disturbed,' Liam growled without lifting his head as a heavy rap sounded at his office door.

He returned to glowering at his latest set of patient notes—the words swimming before his eyes for the third time in the past post-midnight hour—before the door swung open. He lifted his head furiously.

'I repeat—'

'I heard what you said.' Her voice—the last one he'd ever expected to hear again—cut him off breezily. Almost amused. And his words tailed off.

He wasn't even sure if he kept breathing.

'Talia.'

It was a less of a greeting and more of a prayer. At least, that was how it sounded in Liam's head. The woman he was trying to keep from haunting every last corner of his brain was now standing, in the very real flesh, in his office.

All at once he was aware of a good many things, not least being his uncharacteristically unkempt appearance and his office's uncommon messy state.

What the hell was she doing in North Carolina?

What the hell was she doing in his office?

He didn't realise he'd actually voiced the questions aloud—bitten out, if he was honest—until he heard Talia begin to answer them.

'I came to see you.' Her voice even managed to convey a light shrug. As if the answer should be obvious. 'I figured flying up here was the easiest option, especially since you didn't seem to be picking up your phone.'

'I've been busy.'

His tone was more defensive than he might have intended, and he cursed himself for his weakness. So much for never allowing himself to be vulnerable again. But, then, he hadn't expected her to be standing in this office again. Her very presence was like a filter pouring colour into every inch of his drab, grey world.

Just like she always had.

It made something scrape inside him—as though this was somehow further proof of just how wrong he was for her. Surely she could see that as clearly as he could?

Yet she seemed oblivious. Instead, in typical Talia fashion, she almost seemed to shimmer across the room as she swept his notes neatly and efficiently from the only other chair and into their appropriate files in the tall cabinet, before sitting gracefully on the incommodious scratchy wool-upholstered chair.

'I've heard how busy you've been,' she said, almost conversationally, though he knew he wasn't wrong in detecting a note of censure in there. And something else. Concern. 'Taking on case after case, researching, studying; practically living here in your office or in that operating room.'

'It's called work.'

She shook her head.

'It's called avoidance, Liam. You and I both know it. Days filled with back-to-back surgeries, nights filled with working on new cases, and only the minimum amount of sleep you need to stay on top of your game. You're throwing yourself into work to avoid thinking about what happened between us—and you're driving yourself to exhaustion in the process.'

He hated the way she could read him so easily. He, who was meant to be inscrutable. Composed. One tug from this woman and he would unravel right there and then. Right into that deep, pitch-black abyss, on the brink of which he was teetering.

But he wouldn't look down. He couldn't. Because if he did, he was afraid he might topple. The chief had just imposed three days of forced holiday on him, and he had no damn idea how he was going to fill his days, just to keep his mind off the woman now standing right in front of him.

'I don't have time for this, Talia,' he snarled. 'What are you doing here?'

She looked less than impressed. She certainly didn't look intimidated.

'I'm here to be with you.'

Her response was so succinct, so unexpected that for a moment Liam thought his heart had actually stopped beating. For one long, long moment there was silence and then he became aware of a slow whistling sound in his head, building and building until it became a long shout.

An unending roar.

He had no idea how he managed to speak over it.

'I don't want you here.'

She eyed him curiously. Unblinking yet, apparently, unhurt.

Had he wanted to hurt her, then? He must have. A stab of remorse jabbed at him.

'You shouldn't be here, Talia. Your home is on St Victoria, and it's evident that you love it there.'

'My home is with you,' she replied easily.

And it was the simplicity of her words that made his heart slam so hard against the wall of his chest. Hard enough to cause damage.

'Walking away from you last time...' she paused, shaking her head '...not trusting you with my truth was the worst decision I ever made. And, still, for three years I've been pretending to myself that it was the right one. I was still lying to myself when I pretended that the only reason I gave Nate your name was for that patient.'

'Stop, Talia.' The words might as well have been ripped from his throat. 'This can't help either of us.'

'No.' She shook her head, a tremor in her voice even as she held her hand up. 'I flew for nine hours and on two planes just to tell you this. So hear me out, Liam. Please.'

Their gazes collided. Nothing else felt sure. Or safe. Like the rocks at the edges of that precipice had just crumbled and were slipping away beneath his feet. He had no idea how long they didn't speak and then, at length, he nodded stiffly. A tacit assent that she accepted nonetheless.

'I love you,' she breathed out on a shaky breath. 'But you already know that. I think I've loved you from the first moment I met you. And that long summer we had together were the most incredible months I've ever known. Right up until I got that call from Papa.'

'When he told you your mama wasn't well,' he confirmed.

She let her eyes drop to the floor for a moment then seemed to steel herself and lift them to his gaze right away.

'Like I told you that last time we were together, the worst part of it is that I knew Mama wasn't well. And that's what's left me racked with guilt all this time.' Her voice sounded so stilted and awkward that he couldn't bear her discomfort.

He might not have known exactly how it felt—

after all, how could you mourn the loss of something you never remembered having to begin with?—but he knew how it felt *not* to have a mother.

'You don't have to do this. You don't owe me any more explanations,' he ground out.

'I *do* owe you more explanations.' Her expression was so earnest, so fierce it was impossible not to feel himself getting swept up in her words. 'Even though you didn't tell me…how bad your father was, I knew you'd grown up without a mother and with a father who didn't show much love. To be fair, it was easy enough to read between the lines and realise you'd had a something of a lonely childhood without much love.'

'It was fine.' Liam stiffened defensively. He tried not to but it was too ingrained. 'Other kids have it worse. I've seen that all too often in the hospital.'

'And yet other kids, like me, enjoy wonderful childhoods with loving families.' She lifted her shoulders delicately. 'I just didn't appreciate that fully until these last few years.'

'I'm glad that returning to St Vic…*home*,' he corrected, 'was so rewarding for you.'

And he truly meant it. If it came down to a choice between having her with him and seeing her happy among people who knew her well and loved her, there was really no contest.

'Yet here I am, having spent the best part of a

day travelling, to come and say these few things, which should tell you all you really need to know. Back on St Victoria you asked me why I didn't tell you I was leaving three years ago, and I didn't answer. And then you accused me of playing games, trying to get you to run after me.'

'You don't have to say anything, Talia. It was wrong of me to accuse you of anything. I can only imagine how frightened and confused you must have felt,' he assured her, but she cut him off with a gentle shake of her head.

'The things is…' She drew in a breath. 'I don't know that you were entirely wrong after all. I did feel guilty about my mother, it's true, and my head was a mess when my father called. But now, with the benefit of three years on, and everything you said to me those last weeks, I wonder if there was maybe an element of truth to what you said.'

'What kind of element of truth?' he rasped.

He wanted to say more but no words came. What *could* he say?

'I…' She faltered, then picked herself up again, and he thought it was that strength that he admired most in her. 'I knew I loved you, even three years ago. But I also knew that as much as you cared for me, you didn't necessarily feel *love*. I certainly didn't intend it as a test, but I think that maybe there was some tiny part of me that wondered—hoped, really—if my leaving would cause you to realise it.'

'You wanted me to chase after you to St Victoria?' he demanded, but the strange thing was that the idea didn't rile him the way it had before.

In fact, he couldn't really work out why he hadn't done precisely that. Why, when he'd returned to his empty apartment and seen the gap in his closet, in his bathroom, in his life, he hadn't chased straight after her.

Why he wouldn't let himself feel that love—even now, when he so desperately wanted to—let alone act on it.

She was right, he had always pushed her away. Keeping her at arm's length before she could get too close to him and hurt him. But the sad thing was that he didn't know how to do anything else.

'I didn't envisage you racing to the island after me.' She splayed out her hands stiffly. 'I think I just wanted you to… I don't know…realise that I mattered to you. Enough to do something about it. Call me. Tell me. Anything.'

'I couldn't,' he stated flatly. 'I can't. That isn't who I am. I don't know how to.'

'I know that now.' He didn't realise that Talia had slid off her chair until she was suddenly in front of him, crouched down, his face cupped in her soft—so soft—palms.

'I am my father's own son, incapable of loving. Only I'm worse, because at least he once loved my mother.'

'No, Liam.' Her eyes glistened and he braced

against a sudden wave of emotion. 'You aren't worse. You never got to see what love was because he never showed you. Your father lost his wife and it's tragic, I understand that. But when she died, *you* were born. A pure, innocent baby, who didn't even get the chance to know your mother. You needed your father's love more than ever. But, instead, he was too wrapped up in his grief.'

'You have no right to judge,' he gritted out, even as he felt the heavy weight in his chest rock and shift. It was still there, but for the first time he began to realise that it could be moved. He wasn't sure he liked that. He'd grown perversely accustomed to it over the years.

'I think I have every right,' she argued. 'Because it tears me up to see what pain his selfishness has caused you all these years. How his actions have made it so you don't even know how to love or be loved, let alone want it.'

'That isn't true.'

Except that it wasn't untrue either, was it?

He stared at her as though it could somehow explain to her what was going on in his head. But he knew it couldn't. He couldn't even explain it to himself. It was as though the very air was shifting around them. Pressing in on him. Making him…wonder.

'Three years ago, we didn't trust each other enough to be honest. But I'm changing that because I'm not that naïve girl any more, and because I can. This time I'm here, choosing you. Choosing to be with you. I need you to know that, out of everything that I love in the world—my family, my home on St Victoria, my job at The Island Clinic—there is one thing that I love above all else. And that's you, Liam.'

'So, that means what?' he demanded gruffly, because he couldn't help himself.

'That means I've already spoken to the chief about coming back to my old job at Duke's.'

'You're leaving St Victoria?'

'If you want me here.'

'You can't do that,' he managed gruffly. 'You love it back there.'

'I do love it,' she agreed. 'But without you, there's no point. So here I am. Yours. This time I'm choosing *you*. This is what love is, Liam. Your father may never have shown you love but I know your grandmother, Glory, did. And I want to pick up where *she* left off. You just have to let me.'

'No. You can't do that.' He had no idea how he spoke with the lump l that seemed to be blocking his throat. 'You can't give up everything you love.'

A thousand emotions poured through him. They seemed to sweep from his head right down to his toes. A terrifying deluge. Too hard, and too heavy for him to process.

'I'm not giving up everything I love. I'm simply choosing the one I love most, *you*, over the other things.' She smiled. Shaky, but irrepressible.

Her hands shook slightly beneath his and Liam blinked in shock. When had he raised his hands to cover hers? Had he meant to hold them or wrench them away?

He didn't know.

'I won't accept it,' he began, louder now. Horrified.

Or was it actually something else entirely?

Yet, rather than cowing, his beloved Talia stared at him all the more steadfastly. Her smile chipping away his armour. Making him start to believe.

'Love is—' he began again anyway.

'Real, Liam,' she finished for him. 'It's not just some brain tipsy on a neurochemical triple shot. And I get how that scares you, and that you don't know how to deal with it, but I'm here to teach you how. And we'll take as long as you need.'

'You're asking too much, Talia.' His voice cracked but he pretended not to notice.

'I can only hope that isn't true,' she answered, an echoing hitch in her voice as she scribbled on his pad of paper. 'You told me that words weren't enough. That it was easy to claim to love someone but much harder to actually prove it. So here

I am, following you to North Carolina to prove it in the only way I know how to.'

'Talia—'

'This is the hotel where I'm staying if you want to contact me. But I'm not holding you to ransom, Liam. If you decide this isn't what you want— that *I'm* not what you want—I will understand. I'll go back to St Victoria.'

'Talia…' he began as her voice trembled, but she pressed on.

'I've said what I came to say. It's on you now, Liam,' she managed.

And then, before his brain could even begin to process all that she'd said, she left. Walking out of his office with her back straight and her head high.

Making him respect her show of naked vulnerability all the more.

Work was impossible after that. He sat at his desk and glowered at the open files on his screen, but he didn't read a single one of them. The words simply swam in front of his eyes.

Eventually, when he could stand it no longer, he launched himself out of the chair, out of his office, and out of the hospital.

Liam had no idea for how long he pounded the streets. This city where he'd been born, and that he knew like the back of his hand but had never, not once, thought of as home.

He walked for hours—not that he would have

known had it not been for the way the moon moved in the sky above him. Or the changing light levels as the sun finally began to make its way to the horizon. But all of a sudden he found himself in the cemetery.

The place where he never came because it held no memories for him. It gave him no connection to his mother. She was simply a woman he'd never known.

And yet now, today, it was as though seeing that headstone with her name engraved on it might somehow answer all of those last questions that had burned inside his entire life.

Liam rounded the corner of the building, a vague idea of where the grave was, and then stopped abruptly. He might have known his father would be there. The man had always visited the grave daily when Liam had been a child. It had been his pre-dawn ritual. Why would it be any different now?

He was just about to turn and leave when something made him take another look. A closer one this time. And all at once Liam was seized by the incongruity of the scene. The man that he'd built up to be such a heartless titan all these years was now gone, and in its place stood a hunched, wizened, sad creature.

But it was the profile that drew Liam's gaze. Such an angry set to a jaw that matched Liam's own bone structure, an unpleasant grimace to the mouth, and even the nose threw off baleful vibes.

This was the man who had once told him—bawled at him—that he hoped his son would never get to be happy. That Liam didn't deserve to find joy, or comfort. That he certainly didn't deserve to find love.

How had he allowed this man and his spiteful words to colour his life all this time? Liam wondered abruptly. How had he allowed himself to miss out on so much? To lose so much? To lose Talia?

*You haven't lost her. Yet.*

The voice was quiet yet urgent. And all of a sudden Liam could see the colour and vibrancy all over again. As if Talia's very presence in this city had already begun to infuse it with new life.

He'd already pushed her away once, was he really going to stay silent, too afraid to open his heart even for a chance at love, and risk pushing her away again?

She was right. He wasn't his father. He never had been.

Spinning around, Liam hurried back to the hospital and got to his car. This wasn't the place for him. It was too full of death and sad memories.

Talia was the one who signified life for him, she always had. And surely it was time for him to grab that life by the proverbial horns?

He practically threw himself into his car, pulling the door closed and revelling in the low, powerful thrum of the engine, as if it approved of his intentions.

*Fanciful, perhaps.* But after the decades of sombre solemnity this moment of whimsy seemed somehow fitting.

Executing an efficient turn, Liam wasn't sure how he controlled his speed as he drove up the hill and back to the main road. And then at last he opened her up and let her fly, racing towards Talia's hotel and his new life.

A life he should have claimed long before now.

And every junction, every set of lights, every turning seemed complicit in the plan as they each emptied or turned to green on his approach. The entire universe seemed to be coming together to ensure he didn't change his mind at the last moment.

But he wasn't going to. Because now, after all these years, he understood what love was. And he didn't know whether to be more annoyed or regretful that it had taken him all this time to realise that true love didn't resemble anything like his father's display.

Pulling the car to a halt in the car park of the hotel, Liam covered the potholed tarmac in a matter of a few short strides and headed across the clean—if a little tired-looking—lobby and to the reception desk. Then another lifetime as he waited for the receptionist to call through to Talia's room and then send him up.

But then, at long last, he was there. Standing in the corridor as she held open her door.

'Are you coming in?' she asked, a nervous smile lifting those lovely lips. 'Only I don't think I want the entire floor hearing our conversation.'

He wasn't sure how he made his wooden limbs move as she opened the door wider to let him in, turning slowly as the almost paper-thin door closed and she stood, eyeing him with an expression that couldn't decide whether it was more nervous or excited.

A dilemma with which he could fully empathise.

And at that instant he fully believed everything she had said to him.

His incredible, soulful Talia.

Because when she looked to him like that, and smiled at him in a way that poured sunlight and warmth into every last corner of his blackened soul, he didn't know how he could ever have thought otherwise.

Or why he had ever been so afraid of it.

# CHAPTER SIXTEEN

'I DON'T HAVE a conversation in mind,' he bit out.

She tried, and failed, to rein her heart in. 'Then…?'

'I simply came to tell you that I love you,' he muttered slowly. As if testing the words out, taking them for a spin—those words that she had longed to hear for over three years.

She tried to respond but all she could do was nod her head, some sound caught in her throat but unable to come out. It was like magic sprinkling around them and making the moment all the more beautiful.

He cupped her face, his thumbs skimming over her silken skin almost in wonder.

'I *love* you, Talia,' he affirmed, more boldly this time.

'I know,' she choked out, not sure it was entirely the best response. But Liam didn't seem to mind. He offered a half-rueful smile.

'I always thought it was a cliché, but I think you know me better than I know myself.'

'No, I just gave you more credit than you gave yourself,' she answered. 'Hardly surprising, given how your father treated you.'

'Enough about him,' Liam managed gruffly, taking her by surprise. 'I've spent too long being the man he wanted me to be. Playing the lonely, damaged surgeon and believing that I didn't deserve happiness in my life. In trying to ensure I never turned out like him, I ended up being exactly like him. But I won't be that person any more. That isn't who I want to be.'

'And who do you want to be, Liam?' she asked breathlessly, unable to control the wild fluttering of her heart in her chest.

'I want to be the man *you* see when you look at me. The man who deserves a woman as extraordinary and unique as you. You light up every dark corner of my world and you fill it with colour when I didn't even think it could be reached. You have this incredible way of making everyone around you feel cherished, and special, and I want to bask in that warmth for the rest of my life.'

'You make me sound like some kind of saint.' She reached her hands up to cover his as they cupped her face. Revelling in the feel of them. 'But I'm not. I'm just the woman who loves you.'

'Which is more than I ever thought I deserved. You've saved me, Talia, when I didn't even want to acknowledge how lost I was.'

The raw quality of his words reached inside her, making her feel happy. So happy. It was almost perfect.

'I think we saved each other,' she told him solemnly. 'We fit, Liam. We each need the other, which is why I couldn't stay on the island without you.'

'And that's the one thing I can't accept.'

She froze as his words sank in. The grave expression on his face chased out that happiness she'd felt a moment ago.

He loved her but he didn't want her to stay?

'Liam—'

'I can't accept you giving up your life, your family for me,' he cut in, stopping her. 'St Vic isn't just a place where you work, or live, it's where you belong. It's the very essence of who you are. Vibrant, and exciting, and vivacious. I always knew it. But seeing you here, and seeing you back home, there's no comparison. St Vic amplifies everything that's so wonderful about you.'

'I can't leave you.' She shook her head, not understanding how he could claim to love her one minute and say he wanted her to go back home the next. 'I won't—'

'That's not what I'm saying.' His voice cracked, the mere idea of it almost too much to bear. Something he'd never thought he'd feel. 'I'm saying that I want to return with you.'

'Wait, you want to…what?'

'We'll go back to the island together. Nate already made it clear that he'd liked me as a surgeon. Even if there's no opening at The Island

Clinic team for the moment, I can work for St Vic's hospital.'

'You're right.' His hands moved to grip her shoulders. Not painfully, more like enough to give her heart a thrill of excitement. The hint of a promise. 'I want a new start, Talia. A kick-start to a new life. *Our* new life.'

'And that's back on St Vic?'

'Back home,' he said gently. 'Because being there is the closest I've ever felt to having a home.'

'But your work? Your career?'

'I love my job, and what I do. But you were right, I've been living my life in the shadow of my mother's death. Every move that I've ever made has been part of a quest for acceptance from a man who will never accept me. I can't make up for my mother's life. She was unique, and precious. But her death was as much my loss as his. He has spent my whole life denying me that, while I've been twisting myself in knots, trying to make amends for something that was never my fault. You finally helped me to see that, and I will always be grateful.'

Her hand went to his cheek again as Liam smiled at her, shaking off any sadness.

'You would do that?' She could hardly believe what he was suggesting. 'But your career? You're a rising star here at Duke's.'

'All the more reason for Nate not to waste this

opportunity of securing me for The Island Clinic team, then.' He laughed, but his voice was thick with emotion and Talia found she liked this honest, exposed side of him all the more.

Because it was only for her to see.

'I know Nate would snap you up,' she managed. 'He said as much last week when he asked me if I thought you might take on another case.'

'And what did you say?'

'I didn't believe you would.' Talia shook her head incredulously. It had been a mere few days ago yet it felt like a lifetime. 'I didn't think you'd ever set foot on the island again.'

'I wouldn't have,' he agreed, 'without you. Nothing is worth it if I don't have you.'

'Is that really how you feel?'

It was odd, the way that even though she knew he'd told her already, and even though she knew he'd never say it if he didn't truly believe it, she found she needed to hear it again. And again. Almost as if it was too perfect to be true and she hadn't yet taken it all in.

And so she certainly wasn't prepared when he sank to his knees, right there in the hotel room, and took her hands in his.

'It's not nearly how I feel,' he bit out suddenly. 'I'm a surgeon, Talia. I'm good with my brain and my hands, but words…well, they were never my thing. All I can tell you is that I love you more than I ever thought it was possible to love. And I want to share the rest of my life with you. Every single, glorious moment of it. Because as long as I have you, I know that's what it will be.'

'For someone who isn't very good at words,' she choked out with a wobbly smile, 'you just did a pretty good job.'

'Good,' he managed gruffly, 'because there's more. You've saved me, and you've started to make me whole again, when I never thought that was possible. You make me want to be the kind of man who deserves you, Talia. A better version of myself.'

'You were already a good man, Liam. I just want you to also be a happy one.'

'And I will be—with you. So marry me, Talia, and I vow to you that I'll spend the rest of time doing everything in my power to make you happy. The way you make me happy.'

'I know you will,' she whispered, her hands still gripping his tightly.

And then, before either of them could say any more, he stood up, lowered his head to hers and claimed her lips with his own. As if that, somehow, could articulate all the other emotions that were careening joyously around the room.

Emotions that they would work though in time. They just weren't needed right at this instant.

# EPILOGUE

THEY WERE MARRIED twelve months later.

A quiet but perfect ceremony back with Talia's family and what felt like half the island's population in attendance. The sound of the waves lapping on the shore, the birds overhead, and the steel band at the far end providing a backdrop better than anything they could have planned.

It had all fallen into place so flawlessly that Talia might have been forgiven for thinking it was all Fate's design. The moment they'd called Nate he'd confirmed that not only was Talia's job hers to take back if she wanted it, but that there was also a Liam-shaped gap at both The Island Clinic and St Vic should he choose to fill them.

And then, a month later, as they'd been packing up the last of Liam's items and preparing to fly home, he'd gone down on one knee again and produced a ring box.

'It was my grandmother's,' he'd told her quietly, as Talia had stared at the diamond ring inside.

A vintage pear-cut with split shoulders, it was exquisite. And she'd told him so.

'However did you get it?' she'd asked in awe.

'It was in that box I once showed you.'

'The one you never opened?' Talia had asked incredulously. 'The one with all the photos of your mother?'

'She'd put her ring in it, too.' He'd nodded. 'Along with a note about giving it to the one I loved.'

Talia shook her head incredulously.

'You never said,' she'd murmured.

'I never thought there would be anyone like that for me. And then you burst into my life. Again.' He'd grinned suddenly.

A relaxed, open smile that Talia had known she would never tire of seeing.

'Thank you, Gloria,' she'd whispered softly, loving the expression on Liam's face.

It had been everything she might have dreamed about, had she ever dared to dream this big.

And when, the following year again after the wedding, she stared into the puckered face of her hours-old daughter, she realised that she still hadn't woken up from that dream.

'What do you want to call her?' Liam whispered, awe laced through his voice as he gazed, mesmerised by his brand-new daughter.

He reeled off the three names at the top of her list. Beautiful names that Talia had loved from the moment she'd heard them. But as she stroked the tiny, flawless fingers of her baby she realised they didn't suit her. They weren't perfect enough.

'None of them,' she whispered, still wholly unable to drag her eyes from her daughter.

'None?' She could hear the frown in Liam's voice and a gurgle of happiness bubbled inside her.

'Her name is Gloria.'

Talia felt him tense beside her.

'You're sure?'

'We'll call her Glory for short.' Talia smiled at the tiny bundle in her arms, who almost seemed to sigh with approval. 'I think it suits her wonderfully, don't you?'

'Wonderfully,' he echoed, as if slightly stunned.

And then he wrapped his arms around them, both her and their perfect new baby, and held them tightly, as if he would never let them go.

'I love you, Liam,' she breathed softly.

'I love you, too.' Emotion rang through every syllable and she knew without him saying anything that he was finally free. The very last seed of doubt planted by his vicious father had finally died, the moment Liam had laid eyes on his daughter.

'I love you both,' he repeated contentedly. 'And I always will.'

\* \* \* \* \*

*Welcome to The Island Clinic quartet!*

How to Win the Surgeon's Heart
*by Tina Beckett*

Caribbean Paradise, Miracle Family
*by Julie Danvers*

The Princess and the Pediatrician
*by Annie O'Neil*

Reunited with His Long-Lost Nurse
*by Charlotte Hawkes*

*All available now!*